Indelible Impression

Guardian of the Markers Series

Debbie Grimshaw

Trenton, Georgia

Print ISBN: 978-1-958877-25-8
Ebook ISBN: 979-8-88531-304-9

Published by BookLocker.com, Inc., Trenton, Georgia.

Printed on acid-free paper.

Indelible Impression is a work of fiction. Names, characters, places, and incidents are products of the author's imagination or are used fictitiously. Any resemblance to actual events, locales, or persons, living or dead, is entirely coincidental.

BookLocker.com, Inc.
2022

First Edition

Dedication

Step one: have a dream. Step two: write the novel.

To each of you that helped me with the minutest detail-
you have my gratitude.

Thank you.

I'm awestruck at how all the pieces came together.

PTL!

Chapter 1

ER nurse Elizabeth Barclay burst through the stairwell door of East Mercy Hospital and stumbled out onto the busy afternoon sidewalk of downtown Aurora Springs, New York. Catching the green light, she sprinted across the street, and headed toward her car parked four blocks away. The slapping of her footsteps matched the pulse of her racing heart. Half-way down the first block, her energy began to wane. Teetering, Elizabeth grabbed onto a wrought-iron fence lining the street to steady herself and doubled over gasping for air.

The stubby weeds in the fractured sidewalk smirked up at her.

Great. It's cracked too. Just like my life. Her gut heaved. *Not again.* Covering her mouth, she pushed back the threatening bile and stood upright on trembling legs. *Not here!* She looked toward the street where she had parked and caught the eye of two men passing by. *I'll never make it.* Elizabeth caught a whiff of the sweet lilac bushes that draped the fence and sucked in a deep breath. Her clenched stomach muscles eased.

It's so hot. Wriggling out of her navy sweater, her shaky hands struggled to stuff it into her oversized shoulder bag. *Think. No, not about the hospital!* Tugging hard on a lock of her chestnut-colored hair, she whispered, "I can do this. I can pull myself back together. I can!"

The fragrance of the heady purple blooms permeated her anxiety. The tiny, delicate blossoms were partly opened, and visiting bees hummed their appreciation. *A diversion. This might work.* Enticed, she was drawn under the curve of the arched metal entrance into the open manicured space of Oakwood Cemetery.

A massive oak tree stood in the center of the roundabout encircled by saffron gold daffodils. Its numerous branches, with springtime buds, towered over a statue of a robed monk with a bird resting on his outstretched hand. Focusing on the scalloped brick edges at the base of this island, Elizabeth found her shakiness dissipating. *Why, even the bricks look like little tombstones.*

Glancing at the path ahead, an ivy-draped building with a door plate marked "Office" caused her to hesitate. *I can't deal with people. Not right now.* She skirted past the building. Veering right at the intersection as a woman approached in the distance, Elizabeth widened her steps and shook her trembling hands. *Calm down. Find something new to focus on.*

She absorbed the dense, pale green carpet and was sobered by row upon row of cold stone monuments—a silent reminder of bygone entities. She scanned the names as she walked the paved roadway. Snyder was followed by Jenkins and then Parson. Slowing her steps, she allowed the peacefulness of the surroundings to envelop her. The trill of birds in the trees lured her glance upward. The blue expanse overhead triggered the lyrics of a song about smiling skies. She kicked away the tune and took another right-hand turn. *Right turns going in, left turns coming out.* She smiled. *That old hiking tip came back when I needed it.*

Epitaph-branded stone slabs in shades of gray, rose, and ebony weighted the landscape. Her focus was drawn to the odd smattering of angels, obelisk spires, and crosses. Name after name. *So many people.* Her sense of calm began to slip away. "No." She stomped her foot on the unforgiving pavement! *Ow! That was asinine!* She hobbled a step. *No heavy thinking. Stay calm. Reset your brain.*

At the next bend, smaller, simpler headstones reposed snugly together. Their dates reached into the mid-19th century. Most were a single-named, flat stone placed atop the soil. *1863! Wow. Must have been during the Civil War. Things have changed a lot. No computers back then. No cell phones. Just in medical advan—*

Her heart began to race. She clutched her chest and began pounding herself with one hand. *Why is this happening?* Breathing deeply to ease the rising acid, she exhaled slowly.

"I have to figure this out," she moaned. Quickly she scanned the area. *Shhh. Keep it together.* After another big breath, she kicked hard at a pebble, leaving a scrape of dirt on the toe of her shoe. *Great!* Glaring at all the loose stones in the cracked roadway she kicked another, watching it slip into the grass. Running a hand through her hair and pulling on a lock behind her ear, she tried to ground herself in the moment. *Medical advancements shouldn't bother me. I love being a nurse. So, what's my problem?*

The growl of a lawn tractor in another section stopped her mid-step. *Time to go home. I think I can make it to the car now.* She watched the driver and the red bandana do-rag covering his head disappear behind the hill like a sunset. *That's what I should do, just slip away. Away from the hospital and away from whatever it was that set me off.*

Elizabeth backtracked to the gate and allowed her thoughts to bubble up as she marched to an internal mantra. *Run, little girl, run. Run until peace comes.*

Work—her ever wonderful memory blocker. Work—with endless daily battles to conquer, long shifts, missed meals, aching back, and worst of all, bodies damaged beyond repair. Their broken images followed her home and sometimes invaded her place of refuge. Often the past just wouldn't allow her to sleep.

While she ran, she allowed today's incident out of the internal cage in which she had entrapped it. *A woman with a head laceration, facial abrasions, and a possible broken arm threw me off stride. I remember reading the orders for x-rays, and then I zoned out. Why?*

I zeroed in on the door handle, and then... I was in the hallway. And then—oh no! There were feet near me as I hunched over trying to stop my lunch from coming up. Elizabeth moaned out loud, "Why?" She slowed to a walk. *I barely made it to the washroom.*

"Oh man," she moaned again, quickly glancing around and wiping a bead of sweat from her upper lip as she had done earlier in the restroom. *I couldn't work!* The surprised look on the charge nurse's face as Elizabeth rushed past and out the door flashed through her mind. *Uh oh, I'm in trouble. How can I explain what happened when I don't know?* "Bah," she growled. "My panic attacks are back!"

Chapter 2

A distressed cry echoed throughout the corridor. Elizabeth centered herself in the hallway, walking slowly. The empty passageway narrowed in the distance giving the illusion of infinity. *Who is that crying?*

The frail, almost unearthly voice pierced the silence again. She shuddered. Listening, so intently focused as she passed each door that all other sound was muted. *She needs me. I must find her.*

A louder, more urgent wail came from behind the door to her left. Stepping nearer, she held her breath and leaned close. A long low moan came from within. *Found her!*

Resting one hand on the door, she reached out toward the knob—

Vzzz. Vzzz.

Elizabeth rolled over and groped the nightstand, searching for her vibrating cell phone. *Please don't be the hospital calling.* Squinting against the glare of the glowing screen, she read a familiar name.

"Morning," Elizabeth groaned. "It *is* morning. Isn't it, Jen?" She stared at the closed shades to see if there were signs of daylight.

"Yes, and it's breakfast time," her sister sing-sang. "This is your get-up-and-get-going call."

"Hmm," Elizabeth mumbled.

"You're supposed to meet me at the diner this morning. Remember?"

"Right."

"You sound sleepy."

"And *you* are entirely too chipper," she said through a yawn, stepping onto the hardwood floor. "I'm moving. On my way to the kitchen now. Let me think. I have eggs, and coffee will be ready in ten." She yawned again and, in the kitchen, made her way to the coffee pot and began filling the machine with water.

"Tempting. But there's not enough time. I have to be at work in an hour-and-a-half. How about you scoot over to the diner real quick? It'll give us an hour. Tell you what. I'll buy."

"That's no good. I need a shower. It's imperative. I just crashed into bed last night." She sighed. "Sorry I overslept. We'll just have to catch up on the phone. But fair warning. I'm half-asleep. Just keep repeating yourself until my coffee kicks in. My brain is sort of stuck on a dream." Elizabeth inhaled the rich aroma before sealing the bag.

"Ooh, I love dreams. Do tell."

"Not this one. It's strange."

"Strange is good. You talk while I make my breakfast."

"Okay. I'm not sure I remember it all, but I… well… I'm not positive it was me, but *someone* is walking down a hallway listening to this pitiful cry for help. All the doors are closed, and it seems like the hallway goes on forever. When I… uh… someone finally locates the right door, I wake up, so I'm not sure who was crying or what they needed."

"That's not a fun dream."

"I didn't say it was fun."

"Well, it's easy to figure out. Obviously, it's your subconscious processing your work day, and the screams are your patients crying for attention."

"Maybe." Elizabeth grabbed a mug from her dish strainer and rinsed it out. "But I've had this dream before. Repeatedly. And there's only one voice. So, don't you think there has to be more to it?"

"I don't know. But you're right about one thing."

"What's that?" Elizabeth leaned her elbows on the counter, watching the coffee drip into the pot.

"It's a strange dream." Jen chuckled. "I'm sorry I woke you up. If I hadn't called, maybe you'd have opened the door and discovered who was screaming. Now that would have been interesting."

"Probably not. I usually just wake up." She poured herself some coffee even though the machine hadn't finished brewing. "Hey, I called you last night, but you didn't pick up." She quickly slid the pot back onto the burner and wiped the drips with a napkin. "Out on a date?"

"Not unless a late night at the office counts as a date. No excitement there. Just look at the two of us. Both workaholics. You know, I didn't even notice that you had called until I got home at eleven."

"Well, it was an emergency."

"What? But you didn't say that. You only said there was a problem at work. So, what's up?"

Elizabeth blew across the surface of her coffee and took a sip. "Do you remember playing freeze tag when we were kids?"

"Yeah, but what does that have to do with work?"

Cradling the mug in both hands, Elizabeth wandered into the living room. "Well, yesterday it felt like someone shouted, "Freeze," and I froze. My body stopped functioning. It was surreal. I was in a fog. Kinda like watching a movie, and this scene was happening to someone else." She set the cup on a living room end table. "It took everything inside me to just get out of the building."

"Bitty, how awful."

"The worst of it is, I didn't finish my shift. I just ran out." Elizabeth scooped her sleeping cat from the sofa, nestling the cat on her shoulder.

"They'll understand."

"I don't think so."

"You've never done that before, have you?"

"No-o." The word caught in Elizabeth's throat and ended in a high pitch whine. Her cat pulled away from her, squirming to get down. "Shh, it's okay, Christine." She stroked the cat's soft, gray fur until it settled back into the crook of her arm.

"It's been forever since you've had a panic attack, hasn't it?"

"Two years," she whispered. "Two stinkin' years since an episode." Elizabeth buried her nose into her cat's neck. "I thought those attacks were gone for good."

"Wow." The silence lengthened until Jen asked, "Was this like your other ones?"

"I guess. I haven't thought about them in eons."

"We never really talked about them. I mean, I didn't even know you had panic attacks until after I moved here. So, moving must have helped. You haven't had any since you've moved here, right?"

"No, but I don't remember them being this bad. I sure didn't have to leave work, and I didn't get sick."

"You got sick?"

"Yeah."

"In front of everyone?"

"No, but I about crawled to the bathroom. I think LaDonna and that new guy, Paul, saw me."

"Oh no!" The silence stretched again before Jen blurted, "You're not thinking of moving again because of this, are you?"

"What? No."

"Well, it might have helped before, but don't go thinking about it now because I'm here. We'll figure this out together."

"I'm not moving, Jen. I'm just so embarrassed," Elizabeth moaned, her voice quivering. "I have to work tonight, and I have no clue what triggered this. My career hinges on being dependable, and I left without saying a word. Crap, Jen. My supervisor will be merciless to me tomorrow. What am I going to say? Wells is not going to just accept my leaving without talking to anyone."

"This is your first time, and you only missed a part of your shift. It'll be okay," Jen said.

"It's the ER. We're short-staffed, and I left them hanging. I could lose my job. It's not okay!"

"I know. What I meant is that your supervisor will probably understand because you're always like Wonder Nurse, super charged with boundless energy." Jen spouted in a commercial-ad voice. "But you were ill and had to go home. You may not believe this, but it happens. People get sick, and they leave early all the time."

"I really need a break."

"I told you that you were pushing it. Remember that vacation I had said you should take? You know, to get away from all the stress? You should do it, like now. I wish our office wasn't so busy, or I'd come too. The beach is practically empty right now."

"The beach? Jen, are you listening? This could end my career, and there's no back-up plan." Elizabeth exhaled a big breath. "I don't know what to do, but I'm not taking a vacation." She sipped her now lukewarm coffee. "At this moment, I can't even think."

"Hey, how about I come over after work? I'll leave at five, and I'll bring pizza."

"I'm working three to eleven if they don't keep me longer." Elizabeth took another sip.

"Okay. So not tonight."

"Well, at least, Wells isn't on duty tonight. I have time to come up with some kind of an excuse. If I say I had a panic attack, she'll put me on suspension. Really, I just can't think. This stress needs to stop. And waking up four times last night isn't helping!" She slammed her half-filled mug down with a thud and then shook her tingling hand in the air, sending a scared Christine onto the floor. Elizabeth sighed then stood and meandered into the kitchen. "Sorry, I messed up our plans this morning. And I'm still battling some anxiety. Can you tell?"

Jen giggled softly. "A little."

"Jen, can we just talk later? I need to figure out what to do."

"Sure. But try to get some more sleep. Things will work out."

"I hope so." Elizabeth clicked the power button and slid her phone across the counter. She ignored the cat nuzzling her leg. *Vacation? Do workaholics even take vacations?* She poured kibble into the cat's dish then walked down the hall and headed for the shower.

"Christine!" Elizabeth whined, pausing at her bookshelf in the hallway. "What's with all the books on the floor?" She picked up several books, sliding them back onto the shelf. "We've discussed this before. No climbing."

Holding up an opened album, she said almost in a whisper, "Hey, there's Dad." She settled onto the floor and began thumbing through the pages, serenaded by the crunch of a hungry cat munching on her food. "Oh, and here's one of David and me. Just look at my hair!" She laughed. "You know, back then I thought I was styling." She ran her fingers through her hair. *Maybe I should have it cut again.* She stared at the photo and whispered to the teenager sitting next to her in the photo, "David. Oh, what could have been...."

Moments lost in memories, Elizabeth finally glanced up, surprised to discover her cat sitting beside her, licking its paws. Elizabeth pushed her hair back and blurted out, "It's hot in here. And that stupid dream! Why does it keep coming back?"

Annoyed at Elizabeth's high-pitched voice, the cat darted out of the hall.

"Sorry, Christine," Elizabeth said, returning the album to the shelf. "I've got to get out of here."

Chapter 3

Elizabeth's six-story apartment building was on the western outskirts of town. Cheaper rent and having a handyman onsite were what cinched the deal. Her one-bedroom flat was practically perfect if she ignored her glass block window in the bedroom with no view of the tiny, green space called a back yard behind the building. Then there was the plethora of spiders she had a hard time removing before she adopted a spider-eating cat.

Christine had been trailing her and rubbing against Elizabeth's legs all morning. Within seconds of Elizabeth putting on her running shoes, the cat was waiting at the slightly opened apartment door ready to bolt.

Slightly annoyed, Elizabeth brushed cat hair from the back of her jogging pants. "You are stickier than rubber gloves on wet hands today." She gently nudged her cat back into the apartment with her foot. "I told you I need to get out of here. You just ate, so behave! And no more knocking down books. I'll be back in a little while."

The door had scarcely closed when a loud scream pealed up the stairwell from the second floor.

Rushing to the stairs, Elizabeth heard a deep growl. “Just let me in!”

She double-timed down the steps then cautiously rounded the corner. A clean shaven, heavyset man stood with both hands and a knee on Elizabeth’s neighbor’s partially opened door, forcefully pushing his way inside.

“Hey, what are you doing?” Elizabeth shouted, inching to within a few feet of the man.

“Lizabeth?” Mrs. Krebbson yelled from inside the apartment. “Help!”

The intruder turned toward Elizabeth, his dark eyes reflecting frustration, and sneered, “It’s nothing. You don’t need to get involved. I’m just here for a visit, so you just keep going.”

Elizabeth guessed the stranger stood slightly taller than her own five-foot-eight-inch frame and was closer to “chunky” than muscular. *She’s all alone. I can’t let him get in there!* His professional appearance, the khaki pants and a white polo shirt with an unfamiliar pocket emblem, gave her pause.

"Visiting? Well, it's apparent that you're not a welcomed visitor!" Elizabeth informed the man.

"No. That's not it. I've been told that she's just ... shy. This is a medical appointment, so you can just go on your way." He ran his hand through his slicked-back orange-dyed hair. "This don't concern you."

"Well, she *is* my neighbor, and anyone can see that she's frightened." Elizabeth stood firm, trying to appear larger than her one hundred and twenty-eight pounds. "Let's just say I have community interest here." Then she hollered, "Do you know this man, Mrs. Krebbson?"

"Nah, not really," came her frail reply with a sob.

"I'm not sure you should be here, Mr.... Mr.?"

"Bob Robinson." The man reached into his shirt pocket then shoved a business card at Elizabeth, who stepped closer and grabbed the card. "I'm with Mobile Medical," he said. "I was assigned to assess her health. That's *all* I can say." He turned toward the woman's door and said, "You knew I was coming out for an appointment today, didn't you, Mrs. Krebbson?"

"Maybe."

The apartment door squeaked open an inch, and Elizabeth could see just one of her neighbor's wide eyes glaring back.

Elizabeth looked at the man's card and said, "Well, Mr. Robinson …" She leaned closer and whispered, "I'm a nurse." Then with more force, she said, "And I'm opposed to an evaluation happening here today. The lady clearly is stressed, and I'd suggest that anytime you have to use force to gain access to a patient, you're not going to get an accurate assessment of their health. *Ever.*"

The man opened his mouth to speak, but Elizabeth cut him off. "Mrs. Krebbson needs to settle down. I'm sure I can figure out what's going on here without discussing it with you. You wouldn't want to be breaking any HIPAA laws now, would you?"

He growled, "I'm not breaking any—"

"Perhaps you could come back when she's calmer, and it would be great if you coordinated your visit alongside her regular nurse. A Mrs.—"

"Jennings!" Mrs. Krebbson shouted. "Rita Jennings is my visitin' nurse."

Elizabeth stared at the man. "Yes, I'm certain that having Mrs. Jennings here would ease her tension."

Robinson paused in deep thought, adding no words to the conversation.

But Mrs. Krebbson had a lot to say. "Ye aren't gettin' in today, sonny! I'll call 911 iffen' ye try again."

She's old, but she sure is feisty. Elizabeth bit back a smile and, as Robinson huffed past her and headed to the stairs, she backed up close to the wall.

Stomping down the steps, he growled, "I'm calling the office! And I *will* be back!"

Elizabeth rushed to Mrs. Krebbson's door.

The woman, startled at the sound of the downstairs door slamming shut, blinked back tears in her blue eyes from behind the gold-chain lock. Her stone-gray hair, usually neatly arranged into a bun, hung loosely around her face.

"Are you okay?" Elizabeth asked.

"No, I'm not okay," she sniffled as a tear rolled down one cheek.

"What's going on?"

"Well, it was my annual check-up that did it." Mrs. Krebbson's hushed voice grew louder. "Rita was here last week. She said my stinkin' blood pressure was high. And then she figgered out my eyesight is failin'. Now, they're plannin' to move me into a medical facility."

Elizabeth gasped. "All this since last week? Why didn't you say something? You could have called me."

"I know. But… my eyes."

"What about the building's superintendent, Harnold? He's always around. He could have gotten a message to me."

"Yeah. Well, when he brought me my groceries yesterday, he forgot my cheese. Guess I got all worked up 'bout it and forgot, and he had his building stuff to do anyways."

Elizabeth released a half smile.

The woman continued. "'Sides, Rita only called me yesterday morning. Then that Bob guy showed up here today."

"So, what are you going to do?"

"I don't know."

"There has to be *something* we can do."

"Ye wanna help me, young lady? Ye kin keep 'im out of my home!" Mrs. Krebbson fingered her hanging security device. "He's so pushy, he 'bout broke my chain. If ye hadn't come down when ye did, he'd ah broke my door. I was hopin' Mr. Irwin in 2G would've come to help. He's home, but he can't hear a blasted thing. He's mostly deef, ye know."

Elizabeth stood quietly, letting the woman ramble on.

"If that Robinson fella had got in, I don't know what would've happened." She sniffled and turned her head away.

"It'll be okay," Elizabeth reassured her. "He'll probably send nurse Rita to do the assessment. But if he does come back, I think it's best that she's here too. Don't you?"

"I don't wanna leave my home, Lizabeth. I'm too old to start over anywheres else. Why can't they just let me be? I'm not botherin' no one." Still peeking out of the crack in the door, the woman's blue eyes searched Elizabeth's face.

"I'm not sure how compatible independent living is with certain medical conditions," Elizabeth told her. "If your numbers are high, having a professional check your blood pressure regularly is vital. It can get serious pretty quickly. Have you been having headaches?"

"Yup, all day long. Fer weeks now."

"How about lightheadedness?"

"Now and again."

"Have you fallen?"

"Nah, I haven't. I move slow so I can catch a wall or the davenport. Those durn witchy spells. I just hold onto furniture. It clears up fast."

"Well, medicine can help. I hate to say this, but your nurse is right about your getting more consistent care, especially now that your vision is being affected. If you'd like, I can try to be here when they do the assessment."

"Oh, yer a peach. I think I'd end up hurtin' that pushy man iffen he comes back here alone. Any injury he'd get would be an accident, of course." Mrs. Krebbson gave a long slow wink through the door.

Elizabeth stifled a laugh. "Let's just plan for me to be here to smooth things over. Hopefully that will save him from any mishaps."

"I'll not be promisin' anythin' of the sort. He's due for some aggravatin' after today."

"Well, by the time I arrived today, it looked like you had already been giving him plenty of that."

They both chuckled, and Elizabeth added, "I'm on my way out. Are you okay now?"

"I will be once I set down."

"That should help. You rest awhile, and I know it's hard, but try not to stress over this. It'll only raise your blood pressure more. And we don't need any other issues. Right?"

Mrs. Krebbson looked away without answering.

Elizabeth quickly added, "We'll get this figured out. What about your meds? Have you taken them today?"

"No," she practically whispered. "I'll go take 'em now afore I set to relaxin'. And I'll send word with Harnold to ya if pushy Bob is acomin' back."

Elizabeth took a step back in surprise when the woman unhooked the chain and stretched her wrinkly hand through the opening. She placed a feathery-light caress on Elizabeth's wrist.

"I'm glad you're okay," Elizabeth said, patting the woman's thin hand.

"Yah, I'll be fine." Her voice cracked. "Thank you again, Lizabeth. 'Twas providence ye came when ye did. Ye saved me today, and I won't forget it." She slowly closed the door.

Elizabeth waited, listening for the lock to be re-chained before heading down the stairs to the first floor and to the door. *What a mess. Who is this guy anyway?*

Hurrying outside, she stopped abruptly for a moment in the exterior doorway of the building, blinking at the bright sky overhead, then she scanned the parking lot. *Yeah, he's gone. Aw, Mrs. Krebbson, you poor thing, I can't imagine being forced to move after living here for so long.*

*****

A few minutes later, the curve of the cemetery's ornate iron gate, bathed in glorious sunlight, greeted Elizabeth. The entrance reminded her of a childhood game where two children grasped hands and held up arched arms while others paraded underneath. *Those were happier days.* She smiled and began to hum the accompanying tune but stopped short as the words to the song were processed through adult filters. *A falling bridge?* Her smile faded. *What kind of kid's song was that? Okay, Elizabeth, clear your mind. No bridges. And... I'm sorry, Mrs. Krebbson. I'll have to think about how to help you later. Right now, I have work issues to figure out.*

Having parked far from the main building and, hopefully, far enough away from the possibility of having to converse with anyone, Elizabeth stood for a moment, her face to the sky, letting the sun warm her spirit. Pink crocus blooms appeared to dance in the gentle breeze. *Wow!* All her morning irritations dissolved like a snowflake in her warm hand. Then with an intense stretch, she braced herself and got her body ready to run.

Starting off at an easy pace, Elizabeth made several loops around her original path, being careful to dodge the puddles. Small birds flitted from the ground as she approached. *Sorry, little ones.* She reached for her water bottle. *Shoot, I left it in the car.* She licked her dry lips and pivoted toward the entrance at a full-out run. *Don't beat yourself up. It's a simple mistake. Let the tension go.* The rhythmic pounding of her feet tapped out a beat. Elizabeth counted to the tempo in her head, easing up only when her car came into view. *Almost there—*

Suddenly a loud growl of a small engine ripped through the air.

She skittered sideways, glancing to the right.

The noise blasted from behind an eight-foot-high hedge.

Wiping sweat from her face, she took a cautious step toward the opening in the bushes and peered through the shrubbery.

An older, thin, African-American man, with dust covering almost every part of him, stood in front of a timeworn shed, holding the offending power tool. He looked her way and silenced the engine. His beige work shirt and blue jeans were a stark contrast to his grass-stained work boots.

"Good morning," he said loudly, removing his ear protectors and letting them dangle around his neck. With a smile, warm and wide, he said, "It's a beautiful day, isn't it?" Pulling a red rag from a loop on his pants, he wiped his hands. "I'm Kenneth Greyson. I'm the keeper of the cemetery."

For some reason Elizabeth couldn't find any words to respond. She just smiled back.

The man gave a friendly nod. "I think you were visiting with us yesterday." He wiped a bit of grass from his weed whacker. "We have a powerfully peaceful place here. I can attest to that."

Finally, Elizabeth composed herself. "Yes, it is." She cleared her throat, took a step just inside the hedge, and gave the man a quick wave. "I'm Elizabeth. Nice to meet you, Mr. Greyson. Sorry, I'm a bit out of breath. I just started my run. I didn't mean to interrupt you."

"Oh no," he said politely. "I'm just getting my weed whacker ready for a get-go. I don't mind taking a break, especially when I get to meet a new face." He casually scratched behind his ear. "I say it's always a good day to make a friend. Too many people are just hurrying and scurrying through life."

Elizabeth batted away a fly. "Well, life does keep us pretty busy."

"That's the truth." He slid the rag back through his belt loop while balancing the tool against his leg. "But it's a wonderful thing to see someone take the time to shift gears and make time to enjoy the world around us." He propped the tool alongside the shed before closing the door and sliding the lock. Then he joined Elizabeth as she turned to leave. "It's going to be a nice one. So, you just enjoy the day," he said, walking her back to the pavement. "And you let ol' Greyson know if you need anything. I'm here most every day."

"Thank you, sir."

"Oh, and you best watch out for puddles. We haven't filled in the potholes yet, and after that downpour last night. it's mighty wet in spots."

"Yeah, I noticed that. I'll be careful."

"Have a nice day, Miss." He nodded again before disappearing back behind the bushes.

He seems nice. Elizabeth hurried toward her car. *I really need that water now.*

Hearing the roar of the tool restarting, she glanced over her shoulder, and as she did, she slipped, fell backward, and yelled, landing in one of those pockets of wet pavement Greyson had just told her about. “Great,” she snarled. She drew her knees up to her chest and gasped, her pants thoroughly soaked. Scrambling to her feet, she rubbed her backside and glanced around. *Well, at least no one saw me fall. Now I need a shower!*

*****

An hour later with her hair still wet, she returned to the cemetery, this time to *walk. No psych eval for me. I gotta come up with a reason for leaving work early yesterday.*

There were fewer cars in the cemetery’s parking lot than earlier and not a soul in sight. Elizabeth ignored the now gray-filled expanse that threatened overhead. She tightened the strings to her hood. *Time to explore.*

At the first intersection, she continued straight instead of turning right. *It's the second start to my day. Let's mix it up. No automatic turns.*

The snap of the flag at the cemetery's entrance faded as Elizabeth resolutely pressed on. The birds from earlier had disappeared, and the crispness of the air kept her pace brisk. Shivering, she stuck her gloved hands into her pockets. *Br-r. It feels like fall, but, at least, there are fewer puddles.* She smiled and shook away thoughts of her earlier mishap.

A grave marker with a big number "17" caught her attention. She scowled as memories of herself at that age surfaced. Mostly arguing about college with her mother. "I don't care what you think!" she had screamed. Of course, later that day, Elizabeth had sprawled across her bed, sobbing, and she realized she did care. *But David was more important than anything.* Their plans were made. She'd complete a year of college with him instead of going to nursing school, and then they'd get married. Nursing school could wait. David agreed even if her parents didn't. *Go away, David. I need to think about work, not you.*

Elizabeth rubbed the goosebumps from her legs as she explored this new area. *It's not as pretty here. But it's newer.* Many of the markers were larger and etched with both the husband's and the wife's names. She thought of her father's grave back in Pennsylvania. *Buried in the same town he was born in. His headstone has Mom's name on it too. I can't imagine my name on a slab waiting for me to die.* She remembered seeing the intersecting hearts on his glossy, black stone for the first time. *I wonder if it bothers Mom to see her name there. Does she even visit his plot? I guess someday a graveyard will hold a final memory of me for anyone I leave behind.*

What's wrong with me? I've got to think of an explanation. And I'm sure it won't be about names on a headstone. She groaned. *It's impossible to focus at home, and everything here distracts me. Come on, what's my trigger? Stupid brain.* "Ah-h!" she bellowed, "A little help, please!"

Chapter 4

East Mercy Hospital stood nestled into a hillside amid the poorest residents of Aurora Springs. Medical transports, cabs, and cars vied for space in the circular drop-off zone while a nesting pair of doves sat invisible in a tree adjacent to the six-story, brown brick building. They quietly cooed as the tide of afflicted people pulsed through the glassy doors.

Elizabeth heaved a sigh as the strain of a distant siren began to swell. Taking one last breath of fresh air, she hurried inside with a pseudo smile and waved her badge at the security team. In the artificial glare of the locker room lights, she ignored her coworkers and mindlessly looped her identification lanyard over her head then closed her locker.

"It's going to be a rough night," a technician quipped to the nurse beside him. "There's a full moon tonight."

A glance in the mirror on her way out the door reminded Elizabeth she needed a haircut. Her light brown bangs hung over her dark-ringed eyes. *I should have put on some make-up.* Shoving her stethoscope into a pocket, her eyes darted wildly as she approached the charge nurse's station. *Relax, Wells isn't here tonight.* She checked the clipboard and got her evening assignment. Three patients on stretchers in the hallway each tried to catch her eye as she made her way to the trauma unit. *Yup, looks like he was right about the moon. It's crazy busy already.*

Elizabeth checked her watch then gently tapped the technician's shoulder as she slipped behind him to join in the delicate dance of triage and treatment. The afternoon slipped into the evening in the busyness of IVs, scans, medicating, and charting.

Maneuvering the crowded hallway had become more challenging by a blown light fixture in one corridor. The deep shadows hid the feet of IV poles, and the constant need to scan the floor to keep from tripping over them along with the rising number of patients caused a lot of short tempers.

Elizabeth panicked when, just as she opened the curtain with medication in hand, a patient screamed. Elizabeth jerked backwards and bumped into a cart, setting her heart thumping. *Relax, this isn't your dream.* Taking a deep breath and exhaling rapidly to gather her wits, she reentered the room. *I can do this. Just stay focused.*

Minutes from nine p.m., a co-worker called in sick, morphing Elizabeth's shift into a double. *I know I shouldn't, but my brain is in high gear. I won't be able to sleep anyway.* Pushing a computer station, she entered one of the smaller rooms to take the vitals on a patient but had to take a step back when she saw him.

The three-hundred-pound man in dirty jeans sat with his booted foot up on the gurney with three inches of a spike showing through the top of his boot. According to his chart, he should have been in quite a bit of pain since the meds had not had much time to help yet. But he sat motionless with not an inkling of discomfort.

"Uh, how are you doing, Mr. Ross?"

"I've had better nights," he said quietly, his face showing a slight bit of irritation.

"I imagine so." Elizabeth glanced at her watch. "It's one a.m. Late night at work?"

"Yeah, I do side jobs after hours. I wanted to finish the framing before I went home. I guess I should have quit earlier." He winced as he repositioned himself on the bed.

"If you had, you'd probably be feeling a little better than you do now," Elizabeth said. "What's your pain level, Mr. Ross?"

"Zero," he grinned. "Can't feel a thing. It only hurts when I move it."

"Zero? You must have a high pain tolerance. When was your last tetanus shot?"

"Ah, I got one last year when I cut myself on an old saw, so I'm good."

"I see." Biting her lip, she typed in the information. "Construction work can be a pretty rough business."

"Nah, I'm a baker, but I'm real handy with tools, so I pick up odd jobs after work."

Elizabeth wrinkled her nose and tried to stifle a laugh.

"Hey, is this going to take long? I need to be at the bakery at four."

Elizabeth turned and wheeled the computer station to the door. She released a silent chuckle then turned and said with a straight face, "Oh, we should have you out of here before then. But I'd be surprised if your pain level is still zero when you're up walking around. You may have to stay off that foot for a while. We'll see what the doctor says. She'll be in shortly."

Elizabeth stepped out, maneuvered around a janitor's cart, and almost bumped into Dr. Reggie Whitman.

The handsome man brushed his dark bangs from his intense blue eyes and smiled. His smile and quiet, "Hello, Elizabeth," left her almost breathless. "I saw your car in the parking garage. I was hoping to see you tonight."

Elizabeth blushed.

"How're you doing? Everything okay?"

Elizabeth nodded, and, finding her voice, she replied, "Yes, everything's fine. I've been … busy." She reached to straighten her hair but quickly lowered her hand. "Thanks. Um, I'm pretty rushed right now. Can we catch up later?"

When she turned to leave, Reggie touched her arm. At six feet tall, he towered over her, his soothing voice embracing her like a warm blanket. "I got your text about Friday. Sorry you can't make it. How about lunch on Saturday instead? I'm off until eight."

Elizabeth blushed again and moved her hand to her neck. "Oh Reggie, I'm sorry, but I can't this weekend. Another time?" She moved past him with a downward glance. "I really have to go." She clenched her teeth and focused on the industrial flooring as she hurried away. *Idiot. You like him. Stop saying no.* She stuffed her emotions into an internal reservoir and slapped back the curtain to her next patient. *I'll deal with it later.*

Half an hour later, Elizabeth got the okay for a break and made her way to the small, usually deserted waiting room quite a distance away from the ER. *Coffee.* Standing in a dark corner cradling a paper cup, she found herself wishing for the fresh air of the cemetery. Taking a sip, she hurriedly exhaled the heat. *Too hot!* As she added water to her cup, she heard someone approaching. *No! I just want some peace and quiet!* Slipping against the shadowed wall, she watched two technicians feed some bills into the vending machine just inside the room. *Ugh. It's that weird Paul and that gossip Brenda!*

"Did you hear him defending her?" asked Paul as he tucked his wallet into his back pocket. He picked up a small bag of chips and offered them to Brenda.

"Yeah," Brenda nodded, taking the chips.

"Oh, she was just sick. Right," he said snidely. "You know, they had to call someone to clean up her mess in the bathroom." He leaned closer to Brenda and said slowly, "I'm not saying it's drugs, but I saw Barclay. She was zoned out in the hallway. She definitely has a problem."

"Dr. Whitman has a crush on her, you know," Brenda replied. Both voices fading as the couple hurried out of the room.

Elizabeth eased herself into a nearby chair, unaware of the tears slipping down her face. *Drugs? Where did he come up with that?* With blurred vision, she glanced at her watch. *Shoot, it's late. I hope you're still up, Jen.* She sent a short text message to her sister: *Can you talk?*

Elizabeth's phone buzzed a minute later. "Hey, what's up?" Jen asked in a whisper.

"It's work," Elizabeth whispered. "I thought I could handle a double, but I should've gone home. I just overheard one of the techs say he thought I was using drugs."

"What!? Why would he say that?"

"I don't know. He said I was zoned out and something about me vomiting."

"Oh, that's just crazy." Jen spoke slowly, stressing each word. "And it's just gossip. Ignore it."

"I can't. This is serious. If they think I'm on drugs, I'll be gone in a heartbeat. I'll never work as a nurse again. Oh, Jen, I knew there'd be gossip, but drugs—" Her voice cracked.

"You don't do drugs," Jen said as Elizabeth began to sob. "Listen to me. You're tired and you're upset. They need proof to fire you, and there is no proof. You'll be fine, honey. Take a deep breath. Come on. Pull yourself together."

Elizabeth took a deep breath. "Okay, sis."

"That's good. Hey, it's late. What time is it anyway?"

"Almost three," Elizabeth sniffled.

Jen stifled a moan. "Okay, Bitty. So, listen. It feels bad, but it's just talk. A few more hours, and you'll be home."

"I know. I was fine until a few minutes ago. Now I'm a wreck."

"You're strong. What's that motto? That thing you always say?"

Elizabeth pulled a tissue from her scrubs and dabbed the tears. "Leave the past out of the present, and keep the present carefully concealed."

"You've always done that. You're an expert. I'll bet there's not one person you've shared anything with since you started working there."

"I have no friends, Jen. That was the idea. When people hear stuff, people share stuff. It's like a feeding frenzy here. So, keeping to myself means that I have a safe zone."

"B-but… today you could really use a friend." Elizabeth could barely understand Jen's words between her sister's yawns.

"Agreed. But is the need of one day really worth risking everything I've worked for?"

"I'm not sure. I'm too tired to think, but it's not like you have tons of things to hide. And if you have true friends, they wouldn't be gossiping about you. Hey, listen. You're sounding better. Are you okay now? Can you call me tomorrow? I need to get some sleep."

"I'm okay. Go back to sleep. Thanks for waking up to talk."

"Of course." Jen's tone turned serious. "But, Bitts, your panic attack wasn't invisible. And it's hard standing up alone while the gossip swirls. Think about making a friend—or two. You'll be happier in the long run. Okay, the sermon's over. Are you really okay?"

"I'll be fine. Thanks for the pep talk. Catch you tomorrow. G'night." Clicking off her phone, Elizabeth sat sipping her coffee while tears continued to fall. *I'm sure everyone has heard of my going AWOL by now. Can't keep that a secret. Man, I wish I was home in bed.*

"Coffee, get me through," she whispered. *Well, at least, it's fresh.*

Chapter 5

The nautical-themed decor on the gray-washed shiplap reminded her of the beach, but it was the pastries here that brought Elizabeth and her sister to the Seacrest Café.

The vinyl seat squeaked as Elizabeth slid into the booth and pushed aside the starfish candle. "Sorry I'm late. I couldn't find a place to park."

The waitress at the counter held up a coffee pot, and Elizabeth mouthed the words, "Yes please."

"Well, hello to you too," Jen whispered to her sister.

Elizabeth's glance darted to her sister. "Something wrong?"

The waitress arrived with Elizabeth's coffee, and the sisters placed their order. When the waitress left, Elizabeth leaned back. "Sorry I'm late. The construction cones were all over the place and—"

"I'm not upset, and you look awful."

"Thanks. I just finished a double shift. And you're a grump, so something's not right. Is it your job?"

Elizabeth picked up the steamy mug and sipped the brew.

Jen ran both hands through her hair. "Sorry. My boss is going out of town next week. I got his text last night, and now I need to have all the paperwork together by tomorrow. And there are three closings!"

"Really? Can you get some help?"

"Maybe. I know his old paralegal still lives in town, but I doubt he'd ask him to come in. He's working somewhere else. Jamison loves to keep busy, but this pace is getting to be too much."

"You need to say something." Elizabeth leaned her elbows on the table, resting her chin on her folded hands.

"I know. I keep wondering what summer will be like if it's this busy now. I'm sure I can manage things this time. I mean, some of the paperwork has been started. I use an empty office to keep the accounts separate. It's just stressful having to have all three finished, in triplicate, in less than a day and a half." She sighed. "I'll be okay."

"Now who sounds like an overachiever? Just like you remind me, you can't keep working without a break. Let me restate that. You can, but it's not healthy. You should tell him now, so he has time to hire an assistant." She hugged her coffee mug and took another sip.

"I know. Okay." Jen picked up her coffee. "Let's drop the office talk. You sound better than you did a few hours ago."

Elizabeth opened her mouth to speak, but Jen added, "How does he expect me to make his flight reservations without an itinerary?"

"Uh...Did you ask him for it?"

"Well, no—"

"So, ask him. Sounds like he forgot." Elizabeth covered a yawn.

"He always forgets. I'm just so stressed! Things like that should only be done during business hours not at home on my time. And every time he's in the office, he drops more work on my desk."

"Whoa. You definitely shouldn't have to bring work home."

"I usually don't. But I may have to if I can't catch up."

"Jen, you should take your own advice. Remember that you're a hard worker. You stay late to make sure everything is done. So don't second guess yourself. If he's neglected to give you his itinerary, then ask for it. He'll appreciate the reminder."

"Yeah, but I don't want him to think I'm incompetent."

The waitress slid their plates onto the table. "More coffee?"

"Yes, please," the sisters answered together.

The waitress nodded and hurried to another booth.

"Incompetent?" Elizabeth said. "You're not a mind reader. You'll have to make it the first thing you ask for the next time he throws something at you at the last minute."

"Yeah, I don't know why I didn't."

"It's understandable after a long day and all that work. But you're his only employee. He knows you're competent. Okay, change of topics."

"Good. Tell me about you. How did the rest of your shift go?"

"I'm not going home for Mother's Day."

Silence. Then Jen finally squealed, "What? Bitty, no! You've gotta go. Mom's expecting you. You know I don't handle her well alone."

Jen's overreaction attracted the attention of the returning waitress and the couple in a nearby booth. "Something wrong with the food?" The waitress looked puzzled as she refilled their cups.

"Nope, we're good." Elizabeth said, pointing to her sister, "She just got excited. Thanks."

"Excited?" Jen whispered as the waitress walked away. "Try traumatized. Bitty, I can't go without you."

"Neither of us handles her well. But I can't leave town. I'm on call that weekend." Elizabeth studied her plate, grimacing at the lie.

"You know Mom invited Will to dinner too, don't you? I don't want to spend time with him. Especially if you're not there for support!"

"Jen, he *is* your husband," Elizabeth said in a lower tone before taking a bite of her croissant.

"I know, but I'm moving on. And so should he! Why would he even accept the invitation anyway? And Mom shouldn't be including him. We're separated! Now I can't bring Trent. I wanted the family to meet him, but now I can't. Not if Will's there."

"Trent? Who's Trent? You invited a guy to Mom's? I didn't even know you were dating!"

"Oh, we've had lunch a couple of times."

"I asked you if you were dating a while back, and you never said a thing."

"No." Jen pointed her finger at Elizabeth. "You specifically asked me if I was on a date when I was working late. And I'm not sure Trent and I were really dating when you asked. We were just at the flirting stage."

"So that was like… what? A couple days ago? Okay, so tell me about Trent. How did you meet?"

"Oh, he's the cutest. He's a delivery driver. One day he was dropping a package off and I mentioned I had ordered a sandwich from the sub place next door, and he sweetly volunteered to go get it for me. And when he came back, he had his own sub, so he sat with me, and we had lunch together. He's been exclusively delivering supplies to the office himself, for a few months now." Jen gave Elizabeth a sly smile, ignoring her scrambled eggs and cranberry muffin.

"Of course, and I'm sure the office is well stocked now too. But really, bringing him to meet Mom? Are you crazy? Does he know what he's in for?"

"No, but he'll be okay. He's so sweet."

Elizabeth took another bite of her croissant. "Hmm." *Bringing a delivery guy to meet Mom? I hope Mom lets him stay to eat.*

"I'm going to have to bring him to meet you sometime."

Elizabeth nodded. "Hey, you better get eating."

Jen grabbed her fork and took a few bites of the eggs.

"Oh, there's something else I've been thinking about," Elizabeth said. "Remember that camping trip we took when Mom didn't come with us?"

"Yeah?"

"What do you remember about it?"

"Why?"

"I'm trying to figure something out."

"It was stupid. Mom didn't have the trip on the calendar. Dad was mad, and Mom stayed home. So what?"

"Mom said something to us as she helped pack our clothes. I remember she was staying home to finish paperwork and made a comment about money. Can you remember what she said?"

"Really? That was ages ago."

"Please?"

"All I remember is that Dad forgot to tell her about reserving the site. Mom told him to take us and to go without her."

"Yeah, but there was a comment about money. Remember?"

"Dad said something like, 'Paperwork can wait. The girls are growing up too fast.' And then he said something about her choosing income over relationships."

"That's it! I couldn't remember the phrase. Mom said, 'Income is relational,' which I think implies that she thought work was about more than just making money. Right?"

"I don't know. I never thought about it. We were teenagers. Maybe she meant that you have to work to get paid."

"Maybe. It was weird, though. They never argued in front of us."

"That's the only fight I remember."

"You know, I don't think I ever saw Mom completely relax. But she was definitely less stressed when we were on vacation. And I was mad at her for staying home that weekend."

"Mad that she *stayed* home?" Jen shook her head.

"Yeah. She worked all the time. I always felt her job was more important than being with us. But maybe it was more about keeping her job. As County Clerk she had to do well to get reelected. That was an election year, you know."

"No, I didn't know, Elizabeth. And what does it matter what Mom said? It's ancient history. And why are you defending her? She made life difficult. I was glad when she *didn't* come. We had a great weekend with Dad. That's what *I* remember." Jen finished with a snip.

"I know. It *was* great. But we had all the fun, and Mom was stuck home working. I guess I felt guilty. I know she's demanding. And has incredibly high standards for us—"

"Yeah, no kidding." Jen sipped her coffee.

"Help me out here, Jen. How do you think Mom will react if I need to change jobs?"

"That's what this stupid conversation is about?"

Elizabeth grimaced as Jen set her coffee back down and leaned across the table. "I can tell you right now that Mom will find something to complain about no matter what you do. That's Mom. That weekend we had with Dad was awesome because he relaxed the rules. With her around, there's no bending. She finds fault in everything."

"I know she won't be happy, but I'm hoping I can respond better. And you're right, Dad really made that trip memorable. I miss him so much. Remember his corny dentist jokes?"

"Yeah, he sure loved making us laugh." Jen took a deep breath and took a small bite of her muffin. "The one positive thing I *will* say about Mom is that it was good that she *did* keep her job. I'm sure she never imagined that Dad would die before he got anywhere near retiring. He'd be … like what? Sixty now?"

"Just fifty-four, Jen. I dreamt about him last—"

"Oh, Bitty, I'm going to be late. I gotta go! You got the bill this time, right?"

Elizabeth nodded. "Yes, I've got it."

"Oh, I wanted to tell you, Trent is taking me to 'The Phantom of the Opera' Saturday night. I'm so excited!" Jen took one last swig of her coffee.

"Wonderful. I hear it's brilliant. Hey, I'm going to make cookies later. You coming over after work to help me eat them?"

"Not with all the paperwork I have to finish." Jen's voice lilted. "But you said we'll do lunch at your place on Saturday, so save me a couple. Oh wait! That's perfect. How about I bring Trent with me? You can meet him. You're going to love him. He's great. Oh, I really gotta go." She stood up and grabbed her muffin. "You go get some sleep. You look terrible. See you Saturday."

"Call me to firm up plans—"

In seconds, Jen was out the door.

You'll love Trent. He's so great. Elizabeth rolled her eyes as she stared at Jen's uneaten eggs. *What was I supposed to say? What about your husband, Jen? What about Will? She didn't hear a word I said. Her excitement over Trent is blocking all reception.* Elizabeth picked up her coffee and sighed deeply.

Besides, Mom has already said enough for both of us. Rehearsing a past conversation with Jen, Elizabeth remembered Jen's complaint that Mom had lectured her for going out with her girlfriends after work one Friday.

Jen had recounted her mother's remark in a nasally voice, "Why, I've seen more of your husband this week than you have. You shouldn't go out after work. Your decisions are pushing him away."

Jen was livid. She went out every night that week. Like a few hours with her girlfriends on a Friday was the worst thing ever.

Snapping back to the present, Elizabeth sipped her coffee and muttered to herself, "Well, Mom might have been right. The marriage did end, but Mom really needs to be more tactful."

Then one of Elizabeth's harshest warnings to her sister floated through her mind. *"You had an affair? Oh, Jen. Get some counseling. Work it out."*

Totally frustrated, Elizabeth stared off into the past as her coffee grew cold.

Chapter 6

The overnight drenching rain caused the dark green leaves of a row of maple trees to shimmer in the bright morning sun. Elizabeth hid her tired eyes behind sunglasses as she took a morning stroll through the cemetery. She spotted someone busy near the main building. Of course! She couldn't miss the lanky form of Mr. Greyson. He stood on a ladder propped against the stately mausoleum giving the windows a much-needed cleaning. He waved a red rag when he noticed her and hollered, "You're back!"

Slowing her gait, she scanned the area for eavesdroppers before loudly responding, "It seems this is the only place I can find peace. Odd, isn't it? Visiting a cemetery. Kind of creepy, wouldn't you say?"

Mr. Greyson inched his way off the ladder. "Not for me. This *is* a place of final rest." He draped his cleaning cloth on a ladder rung. "You can't get more peaceful than that."

"No, I guess you can't." Elizabeth smiled and joined the man. "There's no drama here, no people in pain." *No anxiety attacks.* "Using your word, I find it very—restful."

"It sounds like you and high stress are intimately acquainted." He leaned against the ladder and smiled at Elizabeth. "Might I guess that you are a hospital employee?"

"Very good. I'm a nurse. I'm sure you know that hospitals are very busy. I think that's why I enjoy it here. It's quiet." She glanced at the path ahead, ignoring the memory of her supervisor's phone message left the evening before. *I'll call you back when I get home, Wells.* Stepping away from the man, she said, "I only have a few minutes for my walk this morning, Mr. Greyson. It's nice to see you again."

"You, as well." He yanked the rag from the ladder, and, with a snap of his wrist, a puff of dust scattered into the air. "It's a beautiful day! Enjoy your walk, Miss Elizabeth." He looked to Elizabeth's left and waved to someone.

Out of the corner of her eye, Elizabeth saw a middle-aged couple waving back. She turned the opposite direction and walked away briskly, inhaling the aroma of the newly cleansed earth wafting on the soft breeze. *Just a short walk to clear my head.*

Passing a row of headstones, she smirked at Mr. Garfield's, whose name reminded her of the cartoon cat. Elizabeth's eyes were drawn to an ornate, concrete house-type structure sitting boastfully at the apex of a hill. As she stood at the road's edge, she marveled at the structure's detail, the arched marbled entrance engraved at its crown with the name Sanborne. *Marble!* Carefully she worked her way around the smaller headstones surrounding the grandiose marvel. Each had been inscribed with one word, apparently a description of their relationship to Sanborne. Elizabeth gasped when she read the word "WIFE." She checked the back of the stone. Blank. Quickly she checked the other three markers. Two were etched "SON," and one was engraved "DAUGHTER."

Elizabeth moved back under the archway and glared at the mausoleum; her hands balled into fists. *No names? Really? Not even for your wife? Or your kids?* In disbelief, she moved pensively around the monument, searching for names. *You didn't even differentiate one son from the other. Why, this is like an American version of a pyramid!* She pointed at the cement vault at the top of the hill and growled under her breath, "You jerk! This must've cost a fortune, and you couldn't even add their names?" Hurrying back to the roadway, she rubbed at the indentations that her fingernails had made in her palms. *That poor family.* She took one last glance at the monument, her temper flaring. "You may have been wealthy, Mr. Sanborne, but a better man would have acknowledged his family!" She shook her head, continuing her brisk walk.

Studying that monument took Elizabeth back to when she had just turned nineteen, standing next to her mother at her father's funeral, looking at the line of people who came to pay their respects. Each one passed by with words of tribute and sympathy.

A few shared how the generous man had provided dental care in an emergency: "Dr. Barclay, such a kind man." "So gentle." "He always made me laugh."

At that funeral, Elizabeth stood silently, their words mostly unabsorbed. *Dad's gone.* Her mother, last in line, chatted with everyone, taking in each story, the ever-genial County Clerk. When the funeral director came by with bottles of water, her mother leaned to Elizabeth and chided, "If you can't say something to these people, at least smile. This is your father's last hurrah. Nothing will ever match his legacy, so smile and act like you're a somebody."

A bird's chirp from a maple tree brought Elizabeth's mind back to the cemetery and to the man-made shrine she had just studied. *People are unique. They deserve to be acknowledged individually.* She took a deep breath, her eyes flooding with tears that dribbled down her face. She quickly wiped her cheeks on her jacket sleeves as she continued her walk. *This is so awful. I have to find something better to think about. I must.*

In the next section of the cemetery, the orderly rows gave way to a mishmash of markers sitting at odd angles. It was as if the earth had heaved to disgorge itself of some wretched mass. Many of the outlying stones were unearthed and had fallen onto others. *What happened here?*

One man's headstone was tipped so far over that it rested on his wife's stone. The scene evoked a chuckle from Elizabeth. *Well, that's kind of romantic, leaning on one another throughout time.*

As she so often did, she carried on a conversation with herself as she ambled on, reading an inscription on another headstone. "Let's see. 'Mr. Henry Flynn, Beloved Husband and Father.' Good for you, Mr. Flynn. *You* must have valued your family unlike that Sanborne guy."

As Elizabeth hurried along, her sneaker caught on a crack in the roadway. She stumbled but caught herself before falling. She cautiously stepped over a large split in the drive that held water from the previous day's rain. She reprimanded herself. "Careful," she said and slowed her pace, watching for splits in the asphalt before being distracted by another bird call.

She scanned the trees to spot the bird, but something glistening in the sunlight at the edge of the horizon caught her eye. *What is that?*

She went back to the section of tombstones that had heaved into uneven patterns and studied the object from the lane. A thick wire had been twisted into a shape resembling a cross. The cement that had once covered its frame had all fallen away. Years of exposure to the elements had left it splotched with orange scum. *That's sad. The only reminder of this person is a partially-rusted, bent piece of metal. There's no name. And probably no family around to replace it.*

A swooping bird overhead startled Elizabeth and got her moving again. *Wow, so many birds this spring!* She stepped onto the grass, careful not to step in front of the headstones. *Everything's so messed up.* Tiptoeing, she apologized to the long-departed souls. "Sorry, I don't mean to step on you." *All these people were once a part of someone's life. What were their aspirations? I wonder what their families think of all this shifted soil.*

She touched a marker engraved with the word "FATHER" and lightly caressed the cold slab. *I miss you, Dad.* Tears welled up in her eyes again. *Did you accomplish all your dreams*? Then she scolded herself. *Get a grip, Elizabeth. This isn't Dad.*

She stared at the word "FATHER" and couldn't help but touch the stone again. "It was so hard going back to college after your funeral." She glanced at the clear blue sky and sucked in a deep breath. "You always said that

I was made of tough stuff." Glancing at the stone, she moaned as she wiped her runny nose. "Well, I don't feel so tough right now." *I must be stronger than I think, but I don't know how long I can hold it together.* She set her jaw, skirted back around the markers, and suddenly realized how tired she really was.

On the roadway, Elizabeth chose her path carefully over the broken lane. *Times up. Gotta get some sleep.* As she walked, she watched her shadow staying close beside her as a dear friend. Near the cemetery's entrance, she stumbled again, this time over her own feet, directly in front of the brick mausoleum. "Ouch!" She grabbed a bench and barely managed to break her fall.

"Hey there, young lady— are you okay?"

Hearing a familiar voice, Elizabeth turned, spotting Mr. Greyson mulching a flower bed at the side of the building. He stood, brushing the dirt from his trousers.

Elizabeth lifted her foot and massaged her toes through her shoe. "I'm fine." She lowered her foot. "I wasn't paying attention," she mumbled, her cheeks heating up with embarrassment.

"Thinking and walking at the same time?" The man chuckled. "Well, that can be hazardous around here. The ground is mighty uneven. It sure makes for some hard landings."

"Yeah, I'm not always this clumsy. I guess I *was* thinking about something else. I should've been watching where I was going." She eased herself onto the bench. "I'm not sure why, but I'm having a tough time lately."

Mr. Greyson joined Elizabeth on the bench and with a smirk said, "You know, some of the first things I remember hearing as a child were, 'Look where you're going and watch your step.' Well, I couldn't see where I was going if I was busy watching my feet." He laughed. "It's a conundrum. We have to learn to do both at the same time." He leaned close to Elizabeth and whispered, "Did you know that I was a stumbler when I first started coming here?"

Elizabeth shifted her weight to face him. "But my problem wasn't looking ahead. Mostly I was stuck staring at the past. It tripped me up for a good while. It still can if I'm not careful."

The man took a white handkerchief from his shirt pocket and dabbed at the sweat on his brow. "That was a season when I didn't see a future for myself. I didn't even appreciate the value of a day. I think you could say that I had given up on life itself."

Elizabeth studied the man as he stared at the bench. "I'm sorry to hear that," she said and leaned closer, catching his attention. "And I'm surprised. You always seem so… cheerful."

"Well, it was a rough patch, much like the broken pathways we have here. I needed to let some things go, and that took time." He wiped his neck then tucked the cloth back into his pocket. He sighed and offered a smile. "But I learned something important. I had to stand still when my mind was busy. That way the uneven terrain couldn't trip me up." Sitting on the edge of the bench, he stared into Elizabeth's eyes. "Too much looking ahead, or in *my* case glancing back. Why, that can keep you from enjoying the adventure of today."

Elizabeth realized that she was biting her lip and rubbed them together before responding, "Hm-m… good words, Mr. Greyson. But I'm not sure they'll help me. Lately, I seem to be that clumsy kid that trips no matter where I'm looking. And I don't think there's a fix for that."

"Perhaps you need to practice some balance."

"Balance?" Elizabeth cocked her head and frowned. "My balance is fine. I work on my feet all day long. No problem there." She sat back, crossing her arms.

"I'm not talking about equilibrium." He crossed his legs, settled an elbow onto his knee, and with chin in hand and index finger on his cheek, he stared at her. "Tell you what. Imagine you're in your home. There's a pile of shoes near the door and a basket of laundry in your living room. Or whatever things you don't get around to putting away every day. After a while you don't notice everything you left sitting out. It becomes part of the landscape, and walking around them becomes a habit. Let's label those things hazards."

"Especially shoes. I have loads of them." Elizabeth lowered her arms onto her lap.

He grinned. "Good. Well, if we consider this cemetery to be like a *new* home, there are pitfalls you need to avoid. So do what I do when I'm thinking here.

Just stop walking and enjoy the solitude. And when you're walking stay mindful of the hazards. Sometimes I stop and ponder. Other times I walk with care. It's more a practice of awareness. Balance out those moments and you'll be fine." He leaned back, resting against the bench.

"I better learn fast, or I'm liable to end up in a cast." She looked away, "I'm afraid gracefulness is not a part of my make-up."

"There's no question that you possess both refinement and grace."

Elizabeth smiled and blushed. "Thank you, but you don't know me very well."

"It's a bit hard giving you a compliment when you discount them so quickly."

"Sorry. I'm afraid it comes from years of not quite measuring up.

"Well, if I may say something else without you disregarding it, what I see is a hardworking, dedicated public servant. One with a mighty good heart. I think you should reevaluate what you're measuring with. If you're using someone else's opinions, then you might just have to get yourself a new ruler."

"Hey, I like that," Elizabeth said, stifling a yawn.

"That's enough talk for today." He stood and offered Elizabeth his hand. "You look like you could use some rest."

Accepting his assistance, she stood and stretched. "Thanks, Mr. Greyson. That's next on my agenda."

The man accompanied Elizabeth to her car, but every one of his words followed her home.

Chapter 7

Suspenders? Why is he wearing suspenders? Elizabeth turned toward the refrigerator to hide her smirk which faded immediately when she caught sight of the clock on her microwave.

7a.m.! I'm late for the diner! She pointed to the pot on her counter alerting Harnold VanEke to the availability of coffee. The apartment superintendent had arrived just a few minutes earlier to repair her kitchen sink.

The thirtyish, dark-haired man shook his head. "Thanks. Never touch the stuff. I'm more of a smoothie fanatic," he said, slapping his flat stomach. Obvious that he noticed Elizabeth looking at the blue straps holding up his jeans, he added, "These are my granddad's old suspenders. He was a plumber for forty-two years. There won't be any jokes about my pants hanging low."

"Perhaps not, but you might get teased because you're wearing them." Elizabeth took a sip of her coffee and noticed Christine softly snuggled into a blanket on the sofa.

He ignored her remark and busied himself. "These are called slip-joint pliers," he said, identifying the tool, and then continued explaining the technique of repair as if she were an apprentice being trained. There would be no escape from his recitation of a recent toilet repair no matter how hard Elizabeth tried.

She left the room, but when she returned after texting Jen about her delay, Harnold picked up the story again. After enduring his "crappy crapper" remark and other quasi jokes, she forced a sick grin. Fortunately, her sink issue turned out to be a simple clog. As he finished in a few minutes, he spewed out another joke. "Hey, you know little Serese on the fifth floor? She's, like, eight years old. She told me a good one. What's brown and sticky?"

Staring at her sleeping cat, Elizabeth absentmindedly replied, "I don't know."

"A stick." He laughed. "It's so simple, it's funny."

Elizabeth looked at him, her mind focusing on her neighbor downstairs. "I'm really worried about Mrs. Krebbson. Did you hear that they're trying to make her move? And what can we do about the guy who tried to force his way into her apartment?"

Harnold's eyes clouded as he repressed a scowl. "Yeah, she told me. I'm supposed to be on high alert in case he returns. He sounds like a nut job."

"He was definitely making some power moves. You might need to fix her chain lock."

Harnold repacked his bag. "I already tightened it for her when I dropped off her cheese. And no one is taking her anywhere, not without talking to me." Walking to the door, he paused. "Mrs. K. said that she wants you there if that guy comes back. You okay with that?"

"Yes, I'd like to help, if I can." Elizabeth's eyes widened a bit. "Although I do think she needs to have a complete evaluation. I'm not sure how they'll do that with her being so reclusive."

"Yeah. She's a sweet old lady, but nobody's going to mess with her. I'm watching. Ya know, she was still pretty shook up when I saw her. Never seen her like that. I can't imagine what would have happened if you hadn't been there. Well, I'm glad you're willing to help." Motioning at the open door he said, "I gotta go. I gotta toilet job upstairs. The kids flushed a fish down it last night."

"Must have been a big one."

"Nope, it was a stuffed toy." He winked and slipped out the door.

Elizabeth grabbed her handbag and tossed some food into Christine's dish before zipping downstairs to the second floor. As she passed Mrs. Krebbson's apartment, a familiar eyeball was peeking out.

"Morning Lizabeth," Mrs. Krebbson said. "Looks like we'll be gettin' some rain out there today." Her eye widened, almost with a hint of a smile. "Ye might wanna go back and fetch an umbrella."

Although late for that appointment, Elizabeth felt she had to stop. "I'm all set. I have one in my car. And I think the rain will hold off for a little bit. Any news of another appointment?"

"Nah, not yet."

"Well, that's surprising. It seemed pretty urgent. And you haven't heard from your nurse yet either?"

"Nope."

"Maybe you should call her today and see if she knows what the plan is." Elizabeth took a step closer to the stairs. "I'm sorry, Mrs. Krebbson. I have to run. I'm late. I'll stop back later to see if you've scheduled anything. Please call me or send Harnold if there's any trouble."

"I will. Thank ye, Lizabeth."

In seconds, Elizabeth flew down the stairs and raced to her car. *This is great. I'm not even winded. Must be all that extra walking.*

*****

Halfway to the diner, Elizabeth's phone pinged, and a text arrived from Jen. "Can't make it. Jamison called and asked me to get right in. Catch you later."

Shoot. Well, I can grab a bite later. I guess I have time to take a quick walk before I do laundry. She signaled her change of direction and headed to the cemetery.

A few minutes into her walk, she heard something halfway between a whistle and a hum. Elizabeth topped the next slope and quickly scampered up beside the "tune maker," matching step for step the stride of the limber seventyish groundskeeper.

"Good morning, sir," she sang.

"Well, good morning to you, Miss Elizabeth. You look well-rested and balanced." Mr. Greyson slowed his pace.

"I am. I got the sleep I needed, but I'm not sure my balance is any better today."

"Oh?" With deep concern etched in his face, he offered her his arm. "Hold onto me, and we'll slow the pace a bit."

"No, not like that," she said, gently touching his sleeve. "I'm okay. Let's just walk."

They walked slowly in step, his stride shortened to match hers.

"Life does have a way of chucking us to the ground," he said, smiling. "On those kind of days, we just have to wrestle ourselves back up on top."

Elizabeth smiled. "You sure have some interesting sayings. Have you always lived in Aurora Springs?"

"No, I was raised in Virginia, one of five boys. I'm sure my granny had a good deal of influence on my phraseology." He chuckled. "And my wordiness? Well, that comes from twenty-six years of teaching."

"A teacher! Wonderful. What subject did you teach?" She shooed a pesky fly off her arm.

"I started out teaching whatever I could get. When I moved up north, I found I was partial to fifth graders."

"I can see by your face that you enjoyed it."

"That, I did," he replied.

Elizabeth's eyes slid up the hill to a tall headstone. "Something in this cemetery really bothers me." He waited silently. "Mr. Sanborne and his monument … or should I call it a shrine?" She scowled.

"Yes. That is bothersome."

"It's like his family didn't hold any value to him. Like … he only cared about making himself larger."

"I feel sad about someone like that." Mr. Greyson scratched his forehead. "If it makes you feel any better, his wife's name was Emily, his daughter was Rose, son number one was Theodore, and son number two was Thomas."

"How do you know that?"

"Their names are in the office books. I also know his family died together before he did. Sure, must have been hard on him."

"Oh." She was quiet for a moment. "Well, that helps, but only a little. I mean when people feel discounted… as if they're less than someone else because they could never measure up. How can I… I mean, how can people deal with that?"

"Miss Elizabeth, I'll have you know that your deeds *are* your monuments."

In deep thought, she absorbed his words. "That's powerful. Thank you."

Scanning the horizon, she noticed multiple lines of tombstones. It appeared that she and the caretaker were standing on a hill surrounded by an army of marbled soldiers. "Just how big is this cemetery, Mr. Greyson?"

He stopped mid-step and looked down the slope. "We have a hundred-and-one acres of bygone denizens. And that's a lot of restful souls."

"Wow! A hundred-and-one acres? It's bigger than I imagined. Have you worked here very long?"

"Oh, my yes. Quite a while now." He slid his hand down to a red cotton bandana hanging out of his side pocket and fingered the cloth. "I've worked here nigh on fifteen years."

"That's a long time. You like it then? I mean, caring for the cemetery."

He hiked up the waist of his denim dungarees until the hem almost topped his work boots. "I find this place comforting."

"Me too! I mean, after seeing so many movies with cemeteries, I never expected to feel— well, so at home here."

"Humph, those movies." he shook his head. "They're all drama just to scare folks. People don't see that cemeteries are—well … cemeteries are a home for all these tombstones. Each headstone is a reminder of someone who's now gone. That's a fact, whatever your belief is. Each life was shared with others. Some left an indelible impression while others barely left a shadow. They're all important, though. There's no favoritism here. This is their home now, and I enjoy being the guardian of their markers."

"Guardian of the markers," Elizabeth repeated under her breath. She sighed. "I doubt I shall ever amount to more than a shadow, but I *am* an important shadow to my family."

"Now you're beginning to grasp my heart for this place. Take a look at Edna here," Mr. Greyson said, pointing at a small rectangular slab pushed flat into the soil. "There's just a date. No 'wife' or 'mother' written. No last name or age. Just Edna. But her shadow lives on here. Why? Because I've read her name. I've seen her weathered marker, and I've wondered about her life while I've trimmed the grass. Edna once was, and now she still is, at least her shadow is …" He shuffled then pointed to his temple. "… in here."

Taking her arm, they walked on.

"You, Miss Elizabeth," he continued, "care for many people in your job. You have probably saved hundreds of lives."

"Well, a few anyway." Elizabeth admitted as they stopped in the shade of a tall elm.

Mr. Greyson rubbed the back of his neck. "When you die, you might not have an event to attach to your headstone like 'first woman in space' or 'inventor of penicillin,' but that's not important. You, Miss Elizabeth, have already made many indelible impressions. Whether you know it or not, you are more than a shadow."

Elizabeth glanced up at the beautiful elm leaves as tears welled in her eyes.

"Young lady, you are lovely company, but I best be letting you enjoy your walk."

As Mr. Greyson slowly walked away, Elizabeth caught up to the man, hugging him gently from behind. "Thank you so much for your kind words. And thank you for being such a good guardian." Wiping tears from her eyes she added, "I *will* enjoy my walk very much!"

Taking a deep breath of the fresh, clean air, she decided to walk on a more familiar loop. *Indelible impressions.* She began reading the headstones as she sauntered in the opposite direction of Mr. Greyson. She scrutinized every marker, even those in the shadows, noticing many were moss covered or stained a blackish-green. A few steps farther, she stopped and shouted, "Mr. Greyson!"

In seconds, the man, panting to catch his breath and with his hand on his heart, asked, "Miss Elizabeth, are you all right?"

She pointed to two rows back at a large, gray, granite grave marker with the names of Kenneth Greyson, wife Marie, and the name "Kennedy" bathed in sunlight.

"Marie and Kennedy died on the same day almost fifteen years ago," she said. "Is this your family?"

He moved closer and gently took hold of her arm. After a moment he replied, "Yes, my dear girl. This is where my beautiful wife and precious daughter rest." His eyes glistened with tears. "Let me tell you before you ask. It was a fire and neither one survived."

Elizabeth spoke, her hand covering her mouth. "Oh no, I'm so sorry."

"Thank you. It was a long time ago." He stared at the ground and sniffled.

She shook her head. "I can't imagine how difficult that must have been."

He nodded. "Oh, it was very hard. There was pain and guilt at not being there to save them. And I just couldn't get past the 'what ifs.' You know, our bodies have a very special design. They are able to bring the poison of hurt to the surface, but if we ignore it, it's like we've covered it with a bandage. Wounds fester and grow deeper if we don't deal with the pain. At first, I'd occasionally pull off the scab to let some poison out. And in my ignorance, I splashed others with my anger."

Elizabeth patted his hand that still rested on her arm and just stared, not knowing what to say.

"True healing comes from deep within— from our core. I finally realized that I couldn't change things. They weren't coming back. I had to let go. I guess what I really had to do was to learn how to forgive myself."

"I'm so very sorry."

"Thank you, my dear. I'm okay now." He squeezed her arm. "It's just like I told you before. I wouldn't be enjoying what today offered if I continued to wallow in yesterday's pain."

Elizabeth released a very weak smile.

"My Marie and my little Kennedy, they are always with me in here." Mr. Greyson touched his chest. "Before I worked here, I visited my family's plots and kept them nice. I got to know the guys working here pretty well, and one day they asked me if I'd lend them a hand."

"So, you've been working at the cemetery ever since?"

Mr. Greyson nodded. "Yes, and that led to another discovery," he said with a twinkle.

"What was that?"

"I realized that the biggest blessing in life is in serving and caring for others." Mr. Greyson looked toward the tombstone bearing his name. "My healing truly began when I looked beyond myself and noticed that I wasn't the only person suffering. There's a whole world of hurting out there. And if I take time to listen, I mean to really listen and look beyond the hurting folks' outer shells, then I can share a bit of their burden. What joy that brings to a person in pain."

He paused and, spotting a man walking the other direction, he waved. "Now my dear, I should get back to work."

"Oh, of course, "Elizabeth apologized. "Sorry to keep you. I was just so shocked."

Mr. Greyson leaned close to her ear and whispered, "Don't be sorry. I like thinking of my Marie and my sweet daughter. They're in good hands until we're together again." Then with a quiet tune on his lips, he sauntered away.

Chapter 8

Jenny's giggle echoed down the hallway as Trent walked out of Elizabeth's apartment. "Isn't he scrumptious," she said to Elizabeth as soon as the door clicked shut.

"I...he's... he's something alright." Elizabeth turned back to her kitchen counter and bagged leftover cookies.

"He's so thoughtful." Jen 's foot tapped repeatedly against the rung of the kitchen stool where she had just planted herself. "How many guys would go out to get the air conditioning running in the car so that I'd be more comfortable?"

"I can see you're enamored."

"Yeah, I can't believe we met in college."

Elizabeth stopped packing the cookies and pivoted toward Jen. "College? I thought you said he was a delivery guy that you just met?"

"Well, that too. We just reconnected," Jen said, brushing some crumbs off the island.

"So, you dated in college?"

"Oh no. He was a friend of Will's."

"You're dating your husband's friend?" Elizabeth couldn't restrain a tone of shock.

"Oh, it's not like that." Jen waved her hands at her. "We had a totally different circle of friends, so it's not like that at all. Well… it's not what you're thinking."

"It was just a question." Elizabeth handed Jen the cookies. "Take these with you."

Jen set the bag on the counter. "You do know why I moved to Aurora Springs, don't you?"

Elizabeth wrinkled her nose. "Well, it wasn't for my cookies." She leaned across the counter and bluntly replied, "I thought you moved because you got the job at the law office. And it was easier to adjust to single life without Will around. Am I right?"

"Well, it *was* easier not having Will around, but I could have worked anywhere. No, I moved here because I missed you." Jen stared into Elizabeth's eyes. "I mean, when you were home, we battled Mom together. We were a team, but you scooted out of town so fast. I uh, I just wanted to be close to you again."

Elizabeth's eyes misted over. "Oh Jen, I missed you too. For a moment there I thought you were going to say you moved here to be with Trent."

Jen frowned. "Nope, we didn't connect until a few weeks ago."

"Yeah, but like I said the other day, you usually tell me that kind of stuff."

"And like I said, it was just flirting," she cooed. "But now, well, I like him. But really, Bitty, I did miss you. I'm happy we're close again. It was hard when you left town."

"But you know that back then I had to move."

"Yeah, I know—anxiety, panic. Got it." She fingered the cookie bag as if debating whether to dig in.

Elizabeth touched her sister's hand. "When I moved, we really weren't much of a team anymore. You were a moody teenager, and I was a working woman."

Jen looked up at her sister but said nothing.

"Working at the hospital was a refuge from being home with Mom, but once my panic attacks hit, what could I do? I couldn't hide them. Not from her, and not from the hospital. Talk about pressure. I had a new degree, a student loan, and car payments to make."

"Okay." Jen swiped at her wet eyes. "But it was so hard being home alone with Mom. Then with Dad dying…" She sniffled. "You got away and were living free. I admired you for that. You always were the strong one."

Elizabeth shook her head, "I wasn't strong at all. It was huge. Finding an apartment. Living alone. New city. New job. It was crazy. I was scared the panic would follow me here. Somehow in all the busyness, my anxiety dissipated. I can't explain it."

"Moving away from friends wasn't easy for me either, but you were my lifeline. You let me crash at your place until I found my apartment."

"Yeah," Elizabeth gave Jen a tongue-in-cheek smile. "and I got to listen to you complain about how bad my couch was for your back. But why are you rehearsing all this now?"

Jen continued in a serious tone. "I would've never been able to do what you did. You are the bravest person

I know. I am so sorry you're struggling again." Jen reached over and squeezed her sister's hand.

Elizabeth swallowed hard. "Thanks. I'm glad you're here too." She walked around the counter and pulled her sister into a hug. "You're my best friend."

"Mine too," Jen said.

Without warning, Elizabeth's mind wandered back to the conversation she had with Wells earlier. *Not now.* "Somehow things are going to work out," she mumbled.

"Good." Jen pulled away and grabbed a napkin off the island to dab her eyes. "I'm afraid all this stress is going to be too much for you and that you'll leave me behind again."

"That's not what happened." Elizabeth gave her sister a questioning look.

"That's what it felt like."

"Oh," she replied. "I'll need time to process that. I'm sorry you felt that way. But for sure I'm not moving anywhere now. We can talk about this more tomorrow at breakfast."

Jen nodded. "I gotta go," she said, sliding the cookies into her handbag. "Trent's waiting."

"Okay. You better get moving."

Jen pulled her close again. "Another hug for the road."

Elizabeth smiled. "Sure. And enjoy the theater tonight."

"Oh, the theater! Where's Christine?" Jen asked, looking around.

Elizabeth pointed to the sofa. "Where she usually is."

"Goodbye, sweet kitty," Jen announced with a dramatic flair. "I shall return with news of your namesake."

"I think my cat is the namesake, silly," Elizabeth chuckled.

Jen walked out the door, her raised hand pointing up. "Oh Phantom, I know you'll be singing to *me* tonight. Only to me!"

Chapter 9

By the time Elizabeth parked her car, the dark storm clouds that overshadowed the sky coordinated perfectly with her spirit. The spring day felt more like late fall. She zipped up her jacket and hurried to a faded tombstone marked "FATHER" in the lonely part of the burial ground. Standing in the shadows next to the headstone, she whispered, "I'm back." Her heart mirrored the lumpy, earthen soil. She hugged herself, trying to rub away the chill in the air as well as the irritation building up inside her soul.

"I don't know what to do with Jen, Dad. You should have seen her yesterday. 'Oh, Trent this,' and 'that's so funny, Trent.' Her googly-eyed gaze was enough to gag me," she complained to the stone. "I'm not ready to watch her fawn over him. I'm just not. And Jen said he was Will's friend in school!" Elizabeth cupped her face with both hands and pushed her hair back. "What would you say to her?"

Memories of her father's smile, his mannerisms, and quirky sayings flitted through her mind. "Dad," she said, "I usually enjoy spending time with Jen, but not with Trent there. I liked her husband. I think you would have liked Will too."

She scowled at the cold marble, then her face gradually softened. "I remember. You protected that woman from the guy bagging groceries. He was flirting, and she was flustered. I think they were both surprised when you stepped between them and took her bags out of his hands. You shooed him away, and carried them to her car yourself. And on the ride home you told us that she was a newlywed, and that we girls needed to watch out for wolves." Elizabeth pointed at the marker. "You were trying to protect her marriage. Well, I think Jen has been unfair to Will, but I don't think she'll listen to me."

Elizabeth stiffened as the sound of gravel spitting out from a car's tires grew louder. She shivered in the chilly air and watched an old black car, maybe a Dodge, with an elderly woman at the wheel inching past and heading out of the graveyard.

I still don't know what to do, and I'm too frustrated to think. She hurried deeper into the cemetery beyond the familiar landscape. When she found a trail with unexplored markers, she shortened her steps to navigate the rutted path. *The birds are strangely quiet today. They're smart, hiding from the coming storm.* She pulled her hands up into her sleeves and crossed her arms over her chest as the damp wind penetrated her clothing.

There's not a lot of fun here today. Where did the sun go? Everything is gray: the sky, the headstones, even this pebbled path. She slowed and gazed at the leaves of a tall oak tree, its wide branches a sage-hued canopy overhead. Elizabeth wandered off the stone roadway and closely examined the markers. *These are really old.* She touched the face of one of them trying to find the indentation of words. *Nothing*. Many were like this, so badly weathered the writing was obscured. As if having faced the strongest of winds and storms, they were marred beyond identification; yet, here they were. Still standing proud. *Like valiant warriors*.

She noticed more twisted metal bars. *They do look like crosses.* Walking along the hedgerow at the farthest edge of the cemetery she could see over the shrubs and across the adjacent meadow. *That field is huge. I wonder if there's a back entrance into the cemetery.*

The leaves in the tall oak began to rattle in the breeze. Pulling her shoulder bag to her chest she rummaged through it for her gloves, digging deep. *I know they're in here.* Elizabeth moved to steady herself. Planting her legs firmly on the uneven soil, the toe of her shoe caught on something. She felt herself fall, as if in slow motion, down into the hedge. *Not again!* She landed on her hands and knees, her full body and bag tucked tightly between two bushes.

"Great," she growled, "I'm stuck." Slowly kneeling amid the snapped branches, she swung and hit the hedge in frustration. "Clumsy idiot!" She maneuvered herself up onto one knee and inspected the rip in her jeans and the scrapes on her palms. *I can't believe I did that!*

Something just beyond the hedgerow caught her eye. *What?* Through the broken bushes she spotted a good-sized wooden board lying tipped at an angle in the weeds.

Elizabeth balanced herself to stand and wiped her muddy hands on her jeans. Parting the bushes with her feet, she tugged her handbag out of the shrubbery. *I want my gloves!* She searched in her bag until she found them. Pulling them on over her scrapes and struggling through the hedge, she muttered, "Out of the way, bush."

On the other side of the shrub, she nudged the board and waited. Nothing slithered out from underneath. Pulling a layer of moss and tangled weeds off the top of the board, she wiggled her fingers beneath the wood and managed to yank the plank fully upright.

Hinges? It was a gate! An old gray, splintered-edged gate. Again, she scanned the empty field and then looked at the backside of the cemetery. *Why a gate? What had it led to? Oh, a mystery to solve!*

Elizabeth tossed it off to the side and carefully stepped out into the tall grass. The blowing wind played with the greenery and tousled her hair. She studied the unkempt land between the cemetery and a grove of trees a football field away. *I don't get it. There's nothing here.*

Wow, this ground is hard. Really hard. She stomped her foot, surprised to hear a dull "thunk." With her foot, she pushed aside the weeds. *Could this be a walkway*? She stomped again. *It's solid. Another gate?* She knelt for a closer look. *You don't have time for this, Elizabeth. A storm is coming.* As the aroma of the foliage and damp earth filled her nostrils several tall stalks slapped against her face. She pulled at the roots and yanked them out in clumps, pitching them by the fistfuls in the field beside her.

Dirt flew wildly in the wind as Elizabeth ripped more plants out of the ground. *Hey, this isn't wooden; it's a rock!* Using the flat surface of the square "rock" as a guide, she cleared it until its edges were exposed. As she dug out the last side, the dark clouds began to leak large raindrops. Elizabeth flipped the hood of her jacket up and increased her attack on the strange shape in the ground.

Elizabeth discovered the stone thicker at one end. After she tugged a few more clumps out from the underside, she felt the stone loosening. Brushing the hair off her face with her sleeve, she positioned herself at the skinniest end and slipped her fingers beneath it.

With one big heave, the rock thudded up into an upright position. She stared in disbelief, “It has words! It’s a tombstone!” Years of mud and lichens clung to the underside of the stone. Adrenaline pumping, Elizabeth dug her gloved fingers into the markings, frantically cleaning the stone as the rain increased. She sat back on her heels and read the words aloud, “1904, Foundling girl, 4 mo.” Her mouth dropped open, “It’s a baby’s grave!”

Chapter 10

A zip of lightning coursed through the air, punctuated by a growl of thunder. Elizabeth jerked her head skyward, tossing a fistful of meadow grass off to the side.

A steady rain now accompanied the chilled breeze under the darkened sky. Her cramped knees ached as she struggled to her feet. Snatching her bag and stepping around the broken gate, she wriggled her way back through the tight hedgerow. A howling wind tied itself to the deluge. *I've got to get out of here!*

Mr. Greyson's gardening shack! "It's two sections away. But it's closer than the car." *It'll have to do.* She ran to the tall oak tree, her running shoes now completely soaked through. Stopping, she brushed back her wet hair from her eyes as she tried to scope out a shortcut. Another bolt of white zigzagged across the sky. *Can't stay here! Gotta move!*

Keeping an eye on the opening in the shrubbery where the shed rested, she propelled herself forward, dodging headstones until she reached the gap. She tried to grab hold of a bush to slow her momentum, but missed and caught air. She slipped across the slick lawn, and her body slammed into the wooden shed door. Elizabeth grabbed at the handle and steadied herself, pausing just long enough to pull it toward herself. It didn't open. *Locked?*

Okay. Wait— I remember, I saw Mr. Greyson move something on the side of the door. Elizabeth's gloved fingers fumbled in the cold. *There it is!* She jiggled the hidden bar up in jerks, yanked the cross-paneled door open, and slipped inside. Grateful to leave the torrent behind her, she closed the door and was immediately enveloped in darkness.

As she leaned against the door, the sweet scent of cedar combined with the aroma of the rain-soaked earth greeted her. A small upper vent opposite the door allowed her eyes to adjust to the shadows. She squatted and used her hand to feel the floor along the wall. *All clear.* Leaning her back against the shed's frame, she sat down, placing her bag between her legs. *Please don't have any critters in here.* She pulled off the soaked hood and wiped her face with the underside of her sleeve.

Elizabeth stared at a work bench on the opposite wall. Several bags of mulch had been stacked underneath. *There's a baby out there! A forgotten child.*

As the storm raged outside, tears slipped from her eyes. She pulled off her gloves and wiped at her leaking sadness. *Why is she out there?* Elizabeth scanned the smattering of gardening tools and two dried-out plants on the wood tabletop. *Are there other buried tombstones out there?*

She scooted close to the door and fished out her cell phone from her pocket. The wind seeped through the door, cutting through her wet clothes as she dialed her sister's number. "Jenny, you'll never guess where I am." Elizabeth said, tucking her muddy gloves into her coat pocket.

"Hopefully you're inside and safe from this storm."

Elizabeth rubbed her cold arm. "I am inside. But I'm, ah, sitting in a shed in the cemetery."

"What!? You're in a cemetery? In a—"

"In a shed," Elizabeth whispered.

"Are you crazy? Why are you at a cemetery? It's like a monsoon out there! Wait. Are you okay?" She slowly asked, "Really, Bitty. What's going on?"

"I'm okay," Elizabeth said as softly as she could with thunder overhead. "I come here to walk and think about things. But I discovered something here just before the storm hit—"

"Okay, tell me about that later. First, you gotta get out of the storm. Get home. There's a huge weather front passing through. It's supposed to last for hours."

"Well, I *am* out of the rain. The shed is dry. Listen Jen—"

"No! This is morbid. For Pete's sake, Bitty—"

"Jen—Jenneeee listen. I found a grave in the back of the cemetery, a baby's grave. It's really strange."

"Honey, are you sure you're okay? Cemeteries have lots of graves. Even … baby … graves."

"No, this isn't a normal grave. Well, it does appear to be a normal headstone. But … I mean… this grave isn't actually inside the cemetery. It's on the edge of the cemetery grounds, but it's not near any of the other ones. It's abandoned and covered with weeds. I cleared off the front of the stone, but I need to look around to see if there are any more."

"More graves?" she asked weakly.

"Yes, more graves. The marker said "foundling girl." This is a nameless, four-month-old baby. She was buried in a huge field outside the cemetery." She choked back a sob. "Oh Jenny, who would do such a thing?"

"Well, I never heard of anything so strange."

"I know. I'm shocked." Elizabeth hugged her knees.

"But you can't look anymore today, not in this weather. We need to get you out of that shed and home to safety."

"I know. I'll leave when the rain lets up. I just wanted you to know where I am. I got pretty soaked, and the wind is awful out there. My car is about a ten-minute walk from here, but I'm safe for now."

"I think I need to come pick you up. Where is this cemetery?"

"No. There's no need for you to drive in this weather. I'm really okay. If I start to feel hypothermic, I'll scoot out of here. Oh, and there's something else. I forgot to tell you something yesterday."

"What's that?"

"I talked to my supervisor on Friday."

"You did? On Friday? Why didn't you say something when I was over?"

"I guess with meeting Trent, I just forgot."

"Okay, so tell me. What did she say?"

"She's moving me up to Cardio. I'm out of the ER for good."

"What?" Jen asked in disbelief. "She can't do that, can she?"

"She can. I'm moving up on Wednesday. It's probationary, but it's better than losing my job. She said if I had any more infractions, I'll be out of the hospital completely. Look, Jen. I gotta save my phone battery."

"No. Wait. Don't hang up! You start *this* week? I have questions. This is huge. What did you tell her about your panic attack?"

"I didn't say anything. She did all the talking." Elizabeth sighed. "What could I say? She said leaving mid-shift without notifying my superior was a major *infraction*." Elizabeth copied her supervisor's gruff voice. "And she was implementing a probationary transfer, and another incident of abandoning my position will result in an immediate termination."

"After two years this is what they do?

"Yup. Her exact words were, 'Insubordination will not be tolerated. Do you understand?' And then she told me I could contest it, but it would have to go before the review board. Oh, get this. Then she said, 'I don't know what you're dealing with, but get over it.'"

"Ugh. I don't like her," Jen moaned.

Elizabeth gritted her teeth. "Grace Wells, who would have thought someone named Grace would have so little compassion? Okay, look Jen, my battery is at forty-four percent. We can talk later."

"Are you really okay, Bitty? My brain is on overload with work stuff and now this."

"I'm okay for now. I'll call you when I get home."

"Elizabeth Emily Barclay, I'm holding you to that. Okay? Promise you will call me. What's the name of the cemetery in case there's an issue?"

"Oakwood. It's off Main Street near the hospital, but please don't come. I'm fine. Really."

"If the weather wasn't so awful, I'd be there already. Listen, I better be hearing from you within the hour. And from your apartment, not from a shed."

"Yes, Mom," Elizabeth teased. "I'm hanging up now. Love you, sis."

"Yup. You too. Get home." The phone clicked off.

Elizabeth gathered the hem of her jacket and squeezed out a steady drip of water. *I am okay. Aren't I?* Thunder rumbled in the distance while the wind howled around the door and whistled through the upper vent. She shifted away from the door, back into the shadows.

I can't believe I found a tombstone. A forgotten child... No! That stops as of today. She will no longer be forgotten. She is found! And I'm going to learn everything I can about her.

Chapter 11

The next day, late in the afternoon, Elizabeth changed into old jeans after work and drove her car from the parking garage to the cemetery. *Okay, now back to the grave!*

Driving carefully, she only got about halfway to the back. *There are too many ruts. I don't want to get stuck.* She parked, slipped her cell phone and keys into her coat pocket, and stepped outside. Opening the vehicle's hatch, she exchanged her purse for a tool-filled backpack, grunting as she hefted the clunky bag onto her shoulders. *This bag is like anxiety. You have to carry it, and it's heavy.* Elizabeth adjusted the bag as rising concerns began rolling around in her head. *I was so jittery at work. Why couldn't I shake it? Every syringe bag and bandage stuck to my gloves. I looked inept.* The weight of the bag she now carried seemed to double, weighed down by her negative thoughts. Elizabeth stood at the open hatch and felt her heart begin to race. *Don't count the beats.* When the vein in her temple began to throb, she sat down inside the hatch, letting the bag fall from her shoulders. *Anxiety, you're not going to win.*

Scanning the grounds for a focal point, she spied purple pansies. *Focus.* Forcing her eyes on the flowers, she willfully slowed her breathing. *Don't think about work. Study the rich purple color.* The delicate blooms swayed in the light breeze. *There, that's better.* Her gaze moved to another target. *Oak tree. Nice tree. Tall. I like the color of the leaves against the sky.* She took in a deep breath and slowly released it through her teeth, hissing like a leaking tire, and her heart slowed a bit. *Focus on the leaves. Same shapes. Symmetry. Yes, all but that one. It's already damaged? Spring just started.* She stared at what she thought was a half of a leaf as it swayed overhead. *No, I see it now. It's two leaves together. It's fine. Stay focused.* She shook her hands back and forth and took another deep breath, slowly blowing it out again. *Mm-m, much better.*

Lifting the load as she stood, she slammed the hatch down hard. *Oops. Careful, Missy.* Elizabeth smiled at her father's old expression. *I've been thinking about you a lot lately, Dad.* She paused for a moment. *He can't be my trigger. Right? I mean, he was already gone when it all started.* Elizabeth pushed that thought aside.

The piercing blue sky welcomed Elizabeth after the previous day's tempest. *That's good. Think positive thoughts.* She moved quickly around the puddles and ruts. After wending her way to the edge of the neatly groomed space, she fought her way through the wet thicket to the little grave.

Whew. She dropped her backpack onto the damp, tamped-down grass and blew out a few more breaths. "That's a different kind of cardio." *No. Keep your mind off work!* Elizabeth glanced at the headstone and moaned, "Oh no! Look at the mud splatters from the storm." *Nope. Think of good things.* "Well, at least the headstone is still standing."

She moved the gate from where she had tossed it and propped it against the backside of the hedgerow. Then shuffling around the area, she returned to the little plot. Her running shoes were now saturated. *Looks like you're all alone out here, Wee One.*

Elizabeth listened to the chittering birds hidden in the brush, glad for their company. *I brought tools.* She placed a large plastic bag on the mud spot where the slab had been. Stepping onto the plastic, she knelt and tugged on a pair of fabric gloves. Eye-level with the tablet, she cringed. *What a mess.* After knocking off chunks of dirt, she used a hand brush to remove the splattered muck from the face of the stone. Finishing, she patted the top of the marker. "That's a little better. Isn't it?"

Exchanging the brush for a hand rake, she began digging out the clumps of damp weeds from around the edges. The pile of discarded shoots rapidly increased as Elizabeth pulled and yanked and dug. *You've been back here for a very long time.* Soon, weary with an aching back, she stood and stretched. Adding to her discomfort were her now muddied knees. Dropping her tools and gloves onto the plastic bag she paced around the lot knocking down the tall weeds with her feet. *Double checking.*

Walking back to the newly-cleared patch, she stared at the remaining dark spots on the surface and stroked the top of the headstone. "What *does* the world know about you? I'm leaving, but I'll be back to finish soon."

She arched her back and rubbed the top of her left shoulder. Her twelve-hour shift and weed pulling had sapped her strength. After repacking her bag, she hefted it over her shoulder and began a slow walk to her car.

Hearing the rumble of a mower in the distance, she pivoted toward the sound. *Of course, Mr. Greyson. He can help!* She followed the noise and came within sight of the moving tractor. It was pulling a weighted roll bar to even out the lawn. Dropping the bag at her feet, she stood along the path and waited for him to look up.

Soon he spotted her, drove close, and turned off the engine.

"Are you all right there, Miss Elizabeth?" The man's eyes widened as he dismounted. "You look bone weary." He eyed her wet clothes and added, "And mighty dirty." He scanned the lane, looking in the direction from where she came. "Have you been helping me with my job?"

"Well, I didn't think of it that way, but I *have* discovered something I'd like to show you. I'm just really tired right now. I should have grabbed another cup of coffee after work."

Mr. Greyson lifted her backpack off the ground. "Let me carry this for you."

When she didn't reply he asked, "Now what exactly did you find?"

"Um, it's back that way." Elizabeth pointed. "Just leave my bag here. I'll get it on the way out."

"It's no problem. I'll carry it. You just point the way. I want to know what has you all worn out." He walked close, watching her expression.

"Well …" Elizabeth began and then her voice dropped off.

"Yes?"

Elizabeth sighed. "Well, I was walking back here yesterday, and I noticed the large property beyond the hedgerow."

"Yesterday? You were here during the storm?"

"Well, yes. I got caught in the weather, but I'm fine," she said, dodging a puddle.

"I see. So, you were looking at the property?"

"Yes. Actually, I fell into some bushes, and I pushed my way through, and there was an old gate and …" her voice drifted off again.

"And…"

"It's just ahead. There!" She pointed to the spot a dozen feet away.

"Well, let's check this out!" He set the bag down on a dry spot at the road's edge and gently took her arm. "Why don't you show me, Miss Elizabeth."

They made their way around the markers and stopped at the hedge line. Elizabeth pointed to a small clearing.

"Oh my!" Mr. Greyson exclaimed, releasing Elizabeth's arm. "A headstone?"

"Yes," Elizabeth said, a shiver running down her spine. "A baby's grave." She pushed her way through the bushes and Mr. Greyson followed. Standing on the grass next to the cleared plot she pointed back at the old, detached gate. "That's what caught my eye."

Mr. Greyson walked to the gate and squatted, examining it in detail. "There was some fencing back here years ago. We took it down when we put in these bushes. How in the world did we miss this gate? But you know, our fencing didn't look anything like this one. This is o-o-old," he said.

"Very old. The child died in 1904." Elizabeth sighed.

The man turned and studied the words on the marker.

"I didn't find any other graves back here. Just hers. I was hoping you could help me find out something about her. The office must have records."

"Hm-m," Mr. Greyson said, standing. "Yes, we have records. Of course, I'll help. But you shouldn't be out here pulling weeds. Look at that pile you've got, and you being all muddy and exhausted. It's *my* job to do the dirty work. Why don't we head back, and we'll have Linda, the office manager, search the computer. We should have an answer real quick."

As they pushed their way back through the shrubs, Elizabeth held onto Mr. Greyson's arm for support while he, again, carried her pack. Chipper as always, instead of whistling, he softly sang a tune about the lost being found.

*****

In a few minutes, Elizabeth found herself sitting on a folding chair in the cramped storage room. Mr. Greyson had joined her with a card table between them.

Linda's computer skills hadn't revealed a thing, and it was suggested they look through all the old log books. Therefore, Mr. Greyson had placed a box labeled 1900-1930 on the table.

Elizabeth pulled out a few of the dusty hardbacks, handing one to Mr. Greyson.

"Linda called the baby *an indigent*," Elizabeth whispered across the table, "and she said she was surprised that the baby even had a marking stone. Surely she's not suggesting that the poor are unworthy of being remembered."

"No. I'm certain Linda didn't mean that." He examined a page in the ledger he had opened then backed a few inches away. Grabbing a handkerchief from his pocket, he blew his nose. "I think she meant that the poor were usually buried with a simple cross that a church provided. Marking stones cost a lot of money in those days, especially a stone that size. Someone not only purchased a headstone, but they had it engraved for a foundling. What's most puzzling to me is that this baby was buried outside of the cemetery's marked area."

"I've been wondering about that too. Do you think her family snuck in at night and buried her here?"

"Oh my, no! I don't think that. That sounds like one of those movie plots we were talking about. I think it could be that she wasn't properly logged into the mapped area." He glanced at the black ledger again. "There's nothing in this one. Did you find anything in your book?"

"No, there's nothing here either." Elizabeth closed the book with a snap, releasing a puff of dust into the air.

Mr. Greyson wiped his nose again as Elizabeth drew out another ledger from the box. "There's only a few books to check." Elizabeth held out the book to him. "Ready for another one?"

He took the ledger and handed Elizabeth the one he had finished. "What do you think about placing all the books on the table, and the ones we're done with we'll put back into the box?"

"Okay. I guess I'm just too tired to think straight." She released an exasperated sigh. "I was called to fill in at work after I got home yesterday."

"Perhaps you should head home. I can finish looking through these books."

She shook her head. "No. I really need to keep looking. Ever since I found that headstone, I can't stop thinking about that dear, little child. She may be a nameless soul, but, like you said, her life was valuable. Even in the short time she lived, she touched lives. Someone must have cared." Elizabeth stared at the table, and her eyes flooded with tears. "She was just a baby, and I just want to know something about her." She grabbed another ledger from the box.

Mr. Greyson reached across the table, placing his hand on her shoulder, "How do you take your coffee, Miss Elizabeth?"

"Pardon?" She wiped her eyes. "Uh, just black, sir."

"I'll be right back."

When Mr. Greyson stepped out of the storage room, Elizabeth thumbed through the ledger, struggling to focus.

In a few minutes, he returned with two disposable cups of coffee and whispered as if sharing a secret, "The office always has coffee." Placing the cups on the table, he said, "It looks like we're about halfway through. Let's see what we can find."

Mr. Greyson sat and opened one of the books while Elizabeth cradled her cup. The warmth of the liquid seeped into her hands, prompting her to take a sip. "I wonder why the cemetery would refuse someone a burial if they were an unknown."

"Excuse me?" Mr. Greyson stared at Elizabeth. "What do you mean?"

"Linda said that without a name they wouldn't have been buried her; yet, I've found many headstones entitled 'Father' or 'Mother.' What about them? How would they be added to the computer system without a name?" Elizabeth took another sip of her coffee.

"Well, it's just like Mr. Sandborne's family. The given names are in the computer. Some families can only afford simple markers." His eyes narrowed, "I've never seen one that nice for a foundling. And I'm surprised that it's in such good condition. I mean, it's been neglected for a long time, and yet I could read all the words."

"I did find it face down. That probably kept the inscription from wearing away. But someone certainly spent money on it. You're right, it is a very nice stone so there's got to be some kind of paper trail."

The man fingered through to the last page of the ledger and closed the book. "There's nothing in this one. Hand me yours, Miss Elizabeth." Fighting a wave of the urge to sleep, she slid the ledger over to him.

He opened it and studied the first page. "This looks promising. It starts in 1904."

Elizabeth's urge to sleep instantly vanished, and she hurried behind Mr. Greyson to look at the ledger.

"It does!" she replied. "What does the 'MM' mean?" Elizabeth pointed to the initials.

"Mercy Mission. That was the original name of East Mercy Hospital," he explained.

"So the hospital sent someone over here for burial?"

"It appears that way. This person was a thirty-one-year-old man. Are there others from the hospital in here?"

“Here’s one from ‘MO’,” Elizabeth said. “What does that stand for?”

“Probably the orphanage.”

“Really?”

“Bingo!” Mr. Greyson pointed at the letters “FF.” I think we found her. Look! Foundling female. And she was four months old. This must be her. We found her, Miss Elizabeth.”

“Wow!” Elizabeth slid back to her seat and quietly repeated, “We found her.”

Chapter 12

Reflections aren't always what they seem.

Tuesday morning, Elizabeth, refreshed after a good night's sleep, ignored her pale reflection in the car mirror and slipped on a pair of sunglasses. She bobbed to the beat of a jazz tune on the radio and caught a glimpse of her oversized shades in the mirror.

When her sister had given her the sunspecs a while back, she slipped them on, and Jen exclaimed, "Wow! You are movie star material." *Yeah, right.* Glancing at the mirror again, she pouted then laughed. *No lipstick. Definitely not a star without lipstick!* Minutes later at the cemetery, she silenced the car engine, matching the atmosphere at the foundling's grave.

Elizabeth removed the sunglasses, tossing them onto the passenger seat. She grabbed a granola bar and nibbled on it while exiting the car and retrieving her tools from the hatch. *Man, my leg muscles ache.* Shoving the wrapper in a pocket. *I can't believe that tomorrow's my first day in Cardio. No! No heavy thinking.* With her hands on her hips, she stretched side to side, moaning as the kinks worked themselves out. Then with a hard massage of her thighs, she released the tension in her muscles. *I need to go running again. Soon.* She stood for a moment, allowing the tranquility of the place to permeate her spirit. She found herself singing made-up words to an unknown tune. Thinking of the baby's headstone, she thought, *You're not lost anymore. You are found.*

Walking to the grave, she set down her equipment, and this time she brought a foam kneeler. She pulled the taller grass from around the plot. *Little child, how did you get to the orphanage? Would the church that placed crosses on some of these graves have the answer? They seemed to know the poor.*

A couple of hours slipped by before the buzz of her cellphone pulled her from her thoughts. She quickly retrieved the phone from her pocket.

"Hey, Jen."

"How ya doing?" Jen asked. "Did you get any sleep?"

"I did okay. I'm already out running errands." Elizabeth cradled the phone on her shoulder. She pulled off her gloves and dropped them on top of her bag.

"Errands, this early? Grocery shopping?"

"I started out my day with a walk." Elizabeth turned her back to the headstone and looked in the direction of her car.

"You're at the cemetery again, aren't you?" she asked in a disapproving tone. "I'm surprised you didn't get sick from being out in that storm. Don't overdo it, Bitty."

"I'm not. It's my day off and exercise feels good, Jen. It really does."

"Well, you're supposed to be making new friends so you'll have *real* people to talk to."

"Do you know how awful that sounds?"

"I didn't mean it to sound bad. I just know getting some new people in your life would be helpful."

"Okay." At the sound of a lawn tractor approaching, Elizabeth said, "Hey, we were going to plan lunch at my place. Did you forget?"

"Uh, I still have to check my schedule. I'll get back to you in a bit. But take it easy today. I mean it. You're starting to worry me." Then the line went silent.

Bye, Jen. Elizabeth rolled her eyes. *Walking here is just exercise. She needs to relax.* She shoved her phone into her pocket, walked back to her car, and opened the hatch. *I've got to remember to toss a water bottle into my bag next time*. She grabbed a water, and quenched her thirst, Mr. Greyson arrived at cruise speed and screeched to a stop.

"Are you doing my job again?" he teased, his smiling face relaxing as he got off the mower.

Elizabeth wrinkled her nose at the smell of the oily engine. Smiling back at the man, she said, "Not really, I just think this particular grave needs extra attention. Somehow I feel responsible. I mean, I *did* find her." She scanned the cemetery before reconnecting with his gaze. "No child should be abandoned, Mr. Greyson. And just like you're the caretaker of the markers, I feel I need to care for this little one… myself. That's not against any rules, is it?" She took another sip of water.

"Oh my, no, Miss Elizabeth. It's a powerful thing to witness. There's nothing out here that can hurt you. Please feel free to toil away. But if you'd like me to help; I'm used to doing dirty work."

"Oh no. This feels… so very personal to me. It's hard to explain."

"You were pretty worn out yesterday. Can I ask if you'd please consider taking it a little easier today?"

"You sound like my sister. But that is my plan. I think I was just excited about finding that headstone. I certainly do plan to take it easier today. You know, just being outside helps me feel better emotionally. I don't fully understand it. I guess working with the soil calms me down or something. My thoughts are clearer."

He smiled, "I know. I get most of my thinking done out here."

"But sometimes I'm worried that I might be losing my mind."

His eyes reflected a tone of puzzlement.

She continued, "I find myself… talking to tombstones."

"Well, that's not as unusual as you might think." He scratched the back of his neck and smiled again. "I've seen plenty of it, and I'd have to admit I do my own fair share of tomb talking."

"Really? That makes me feel better."

"Actually, I think it's a way of speaking to ourselves. We know the answers are in here." He tapped his temple. "But speaking out loud helps us to process them." He looked down and said quietly, "After you left yesterday, the manager of the cemetery came out for a visit. I am … I mean *we* are going to work hard to figure out how this little one got stranded out here."

"That's wonderful." Elizabeth smiled and tossed her empty bottle into the car.

"I'm glad you're not upset with me," he said. "You know that I had to bring my boss into this situation."

"No, of course I'm not upset. I know this is bigger than just me. I mean, people can't go around burying bodies just anywhere." She grabbed another water bottle from the car and held it out to him, "Water?"

He shook his head. "No, thank you."

Opening it, she took a long sip. "I'm still going to do some searching on my own. But I was wondering if you'd have the name of the church that placed the crosses here for the poor. I'd like to find out what they know."

"That's funny. I guess I was a little excited yesterday too about what we discovered in the ledger. I found the name of the church. It was Saint Matthew's. I called them right after you left."

Elizabeth's eyes widened. "Really?"

"Unfortunately, the church doesn't have those records anymore. They suffered water damage years ago and lost all their old files. I would have pushed harder, but the rector said they have never placed headstones here. Only crosses. That appears to be a dead end."

"Was that a pun?"

"What? Oh, no, I … uh—"

"I'm kidding. You probably get a lot of cemetery humor."

"No, not too much."

"I appreciate your checking that out." Elizabeth took another sip of water and closed the hatch. "You saved me a phone call. I already tried the Vital Statistic Office, but without a name they couldn't help. But I'm going to keep thinking about it. Somewhere out there someone has to have a key to who she was or how she got here."

"There is one more thing I need to tell you. They're going to be running soil tests."

"What? But why?"

He looked away for a moment. "There's no delicate way to say this, so forgive me. They need to be sure there's a body buried there. Peter, the cemetery's director, thought it might be a case of someone dumping a headstone. Now that's something I hadn't considered. I guess the fact that we didn't notice the gate when we took down the old fencing raised questions for him."

"Wait. Are you saying they'll be moving her?" Elizabeth bit her lip.

"Peter said they'd start with a radar scan. He didn't mention excavating. It is a possibility, though."

"Oh, please don't dig her up," she moaned. "She's been through enough already. Didn't you tell him we found her listed in the ledger?"

"He doesn't dispute our finding, but he does need to make sure she's located where you found the headstone."

"I see."

"Personally, I think she's there. Peter said he'd pursue every avenue of information available. Miss Elizabeth, this changes nothing." He tapped her arm. "You are completely free to continue working out there. Here at Oakwood, we have people that tend to their relatives' graves all the time. Even though she's not your relative, we're okay with your activity."

"That's so good of you." Elizabeth blinked back a flood of tears.

"Things will work out. We'll have an answer in the next couple of days, and it won't interfere with your visits." He headed toward his mower.

"Well, thank you for that."

"I didn't want you to be surprised if you found people working out here." He turned to board the mower but stopped. "Oh, and remember how you were asking about that big empty field past the hedges that enclose the cemetery? Well, I learned something new. The cemetery owns the field. I guess we've got a lot of space for expansion."

"I'd say so."

"Well, it's back to work for me. I saw you drive by, and I wanted to give you the update." He climbed onto the mower. "Miss Elizabeth, you don't have to worry. If there is a grave there, it's not going to be unattended anymore. It'll be under my care now too."

"Thank you. That means a lot."

As soon as Mr. Greyson drove away, Elizabeth hurried back to the tombstone. She knelt at the marker, and with tears trickling down her face, she whispered, "Mr. Greyson said he'll be checking in on you too." Rehearsing Mr. Greyson's words about "Peter," she whispered, "*Oh please, don't move her.*" She yanked out a patch of gangly stalks with her bare hands. "I'm not sure we're going to find answers, but I'm not giving up. Not yet!"

Moving the kneeler to another spot, she grabbed a hand rake from her tool bag and jammed the rake into the hard ground, clearing out a large pile of stubborn weeds. Wiping her brow with her sleeve, she looked at the marker and said, "You know what? I don't need to know more about who you are or where you came from. I can claim you right now. Just like Mr. Greyson said, 'People do it all the time.' I hate thinking of all the years you've been left here unattended. Little baby, from now on you are mine. You were abandoned, forgotten, and nameless, but no more." Elizabeth brushed a wisp of a fuzzy seed off the front of the marker. "I'll give you a name." She wiped away another barrage of tears and declared, "Hope. You will be called 'Hope'."

Chapter 13

"When am I getting outta here?" A sixty-four-year-old patient grumbled as Elizabeth pushed her C.O.W., computer on wheels, to the hospital room's doorway the next morning.

"We're just waiting on discharge papers, Mr. Wentworth," she said to him. "Shouldn't be long now." The strong smell of antiseptic from the patient's bathroom turned her stomach. *Ugh, I still can't stand bleach.* Stepping into the hallway, she shot a hopeful glance at the nurse's station. *Fresh coffee would be nice.* However, squeals of laughter from her coworkers nearby was too much of a deterrent.

Parking the C.O.W. outside the patient's room and without one word she walked away from her busy co-workers. *You're supposed to be making friends, not running away. Shush, Jen!* The monotonous beeping of heart monitors faded as the out-of-the-way lounge that she headed toward came into view. Wrapping her sweater tighter around her chest, the primal infusion of caffeine utmost in her mind.

She headed into the lounge and glanced at her watch: 10:30. She poured a cup of coffee, held the cup close and inhaled the aroma. *At least Cardio allows a scheduled break.*

This lounge was peaceful; seemingly hidden-away, tucked into this back corner. Designated a waiting area for the patients' visitors, it was seldom used. Elizabeth had discovered the quiet nook when she had moved a twenty-two-year-old heart attack patient up here from the ER. Sometimes she had sought refuge by eating her lunch in this secluded spot.

Elizabeth relaxed onto an orange, vinyl, cup-shaped chair. Its retro design reminded her of a childhood adventure at the Cedar Point Ridge Public Library. The theater room had orange chairs like this one. On movie day, she had arrived early with Jen and settled into two front row seats. The movie featured a boy not much younger than herself who fought off burglars. Elizabeth had laughed at the antics, happy he had foiled the robbers' schemes, but later that night she awoke screaming.

Remembering that night so long ago, Elizabeth could almost feel her father's arms around her as he whispered, "Hey, Pumpkin, it's okay." The memory was crisp. The warmth. His smell. The lull of his voice. Back then, she had clung to his comfort until her nightmare fizzled away by her father's love. Now, sipping her coffee, she recalled the image of a shadow at the foot of her bed. *You were there too, Mom. I guess I forgot.*

Elizabeth took a big swig of coffee but choked on it when a technician barged into the room, startling her. He grabbed a cup of coffee and without one word hurried out.

Elizabeth just sat coughing, trying to catch her breath. *How embarrassing. Glad he didn't stay. Wait. I'm supposed to be friendly, not wishing people away. Yeah, but I'm not going to be making any friends by hacking my head off.*

After clearing her throat and wiping her mouth with a tissue, Elizabeth pulled her cell phone from her scrubs pocket and tapped Jen's programmed number, which went into voicemail. *Always busy.* She ended the call and dropped the phone onto her lap. *And you say I need a vacation. Man, with all that's going on, that is tempting. There's no promotion for me to worry about anymore.* She rested her head back on the chair and stared at the ceiling. *But you're too busy to get time-off now, Jen. And you'd probably want to bring Trent. Nope. Not happening.* She looked at her watch: 10:45. *Break is over.* Gulping down the last of her cup and shoving her phone back in her scrubs pocket, she eased her way out of the chair and chucked the cup into a trash bin on her way out the door. *Next up? Lunch!*

*****

Slipping into a packed elevator, Elizabeth, with her lunch in her handbag, patiently endured the five stops to the main floor. When the doors reopened, the mass exodus swarmed toward the main entrance.

Elizabeth stared out the glass doors and smiled. *Yay, it's not raining!* As she headed toward the doorway, she waved to two security men in the hallway and noticed just beyond them that Reggie and another doctor were approaching. *Uh oh.* Elizabeth lowered her head and kept walking. *Just a few more feet to freedom.*

"Elizabeth!" Reggie called.

Wincing and plastering on a fake smile, she replied, "Hey, Reggie." She waved and kept walking.

"Wait up!"

Reluctantly, Elizabeth stopped and turned toward the man.

Reggie sent his friend ahead and hurried toward Elizabeth.

She stepped aside near a wall and set her bag down. *What am I going to say?*

After pulling her into a quick hug, Reggie said, "I was hoping to catch you today. How are you?"

She smiled and stammered, "I- I'm fine."

"You're on the sixth floor now. How's the transition to Cardio?"

"It's good. Not as busy as the ER, but it's—good." Elizabeth brushed a strand of hair from her face. "Is everyone surviving without me?" She pinched her lips together.

"Oh, you know we always manage to get through okay." Reggie's voice lowered. "But there's no replacing you. I've heard several complaints, you know."

Elizabeth stopped fidgeting and focused on his words. "I think you spoiled the techs. You were always one step ahead of them on supplies. They don't like having to restock everything themselves." He leaned close and said softly, "And I miss seeing you, Elizabeth. I miss our lunches together. Can we plan something soon?"

She inhaled his cologne as her cheeks tingled at the warmth of his breath. *Stay focused.* Elizabeth shifted away from him; her stomach tightened at the hopeful note in his voice. She rubbed her fingers across the palms of her hands and forced a smile. "Well, I can't plan anything right now."

"You can't be that busy, Liz. Everybody has to eat. We do work in the same building."

"Yes, but I really need to stay focused. You know, new position and all." She nodded.

Reggie looked intently into her eyes. "I want to read you clearly. Are you saying you are temporarily busy, or is it that you don't have time for me?" He leaned toward her waiting for an answer.

Man. Elizabeth glanced at the door then back again. *Avoid his eyes, Elizabeth. You can do this.* "I can't play games with your feelings," she said quietly. "I like you too much for that." She dared a quick look into his blue eyes. *No. Stay strong.* She averted his gaze again. "I'm struggling with some personal issues, and I can't continue our lunch dates right now."

The man's shoulders sagged and he looked down.

"I'd like to say yes to seeing you outside of work, but I—"

"Is there someone else?" he blurted out. "Is it Dr. Steinburg on six?" His cheeks turned fire red as he straightened his posture.

"No!" She said a little too loudly. Noticing a few people looking their way, she lowered her voice. "It's not like that at all, Reggie." She sighed, "It's nothing about you, and there is no one else."

"I don't understand," he said, shaking his head. "There's got to be more to this. Something that you're not telling me."

"Can we go somewhere else? Somewhere less crowded to talk?"

He shook his head. "I can't right now. But please hear me. This is a struggle for me. I really miss seeing you."

Elizabeth threw her defensive strategy aside and looked directly at him, "Reggie, it's all me. I'm working through something personal. Can I text you later this week?" Her eyes welled with tears.

He leaned back, looked away, and sighed. "I guess."

"I would never want to hurt you," she whispered.

He inhaled deeply before drawing close to her and brushed her cheek with his lips. "Figure it out quickly. Please?"

As Reggie hurried down the hallway, she forced down the lump in her throat. She picked up the bag, which felt like a ton of bricks. *Why now? Why couldn't I bump into him when I have things figured out?*

She hurried out the door and across the street. She power-walked through the cemetery, trying to make up for the lost minutes and to emotionally separate herself from the conflict inside. She yanked a tissue from her pocket and swiped at her nose. Then jamming the tissue back into her pocket, she mumbled, "Sorry, Reggie."

The lush greenery that greeted her with pops of color from the budding flowers helped a bit. *Beautiful.* With her bag secured across one shoulder, Elizabeth jogged past a white van parked inside the gateway, the vehicle's side panel displaying a blue and red media logo. *A news truck? What are they doing here?*

Just ahead of her, she surveyed a long line of cars parked along the roadside. She recognized it as being a graveside service and shuddered as she passed the large group with their backs to her. *Maybe someone important died.* Her hands began to sweat. *Uh oh, shake it away. Focus on something positive.* She turned her attention back to the colorful flowers placed alongside a few of the markers and picked up her jogging pace. Her internal mantra looped through her head as she passed small American flags posted on a few graves. *Military servants. Thank you for your service. For your sacrifice and your...lives. What was it Mr. Greyson had said? Yes, indelible impression, that's what you've left. Selflessly serving for freedom. Thank you.*

Elizabeth looked up just as the sun slipped behind a cloud, and a flood of tears welled up. *What on earth is wrong with me? Get a grip, girl. Stop being emotional. Think, think. What was it that made me smile just a few minutes ago?*

Her mood lifted slightly when she reached Hope's gravesite. Opening her bag, she drew out a small, thickly woven, red and yellow, Aztec blanket Jen had brought back from a Mexico vacation. After arranging the tapestry on the plot, she sat down to eat her lunch.

"I can only stay a few minutes, Hope. My sister's coming for dinner, so I only have time for a lunch visit today." Elizabeth took a nibble of her pita pocket. "I've been wondering about your parents. You know, questioning if they were married or not. Women alone don't always have the support they need to raise a child. A girl I knew in college placed her baby for adoption. She struggled terribly because it wasn't an easy decision." Elizabeth took another small bite of her lunch and found it hard to swallow. "Maybe," she said to the grave, "your parents both got sick and, somehow, you ended up alone." She reached into her bag for a bottle of water. Taking a quick drink, she coughed as the food took a long time to settle. "I probably should stop trying to figure it out. I just really hope that, well—I hope your life wasn't all thorns. I hope that you knew love, that you experienced warmth, hugs, and kisses."

Like a mist high across the horizon, the wispy clouds danced across the blue-gray sky. Elizabeth gave a slight moan as she shifted positions on the blanket. "My morning on six was okay, but I don't think Cardio is going to work out. It's probably the newness of it, but I just don't like it. And I can't figure out what's triggering my attacks. Every time I come here to think, I get side-tracked. And now, because I'm skipping Mother's Day, my mom's coming to visit me, and she wants to stay at my place!"

Elizabeth tossed her unfinished lunch into her bag and shoved the bag off the blanket. "And I just pushed Reggie away because I don't know if dating is my trigger! Where *is* happiness? Am I ever going to find it? I don't want to end up like Mrs. Krebbson, all alone and hiding from the world." Elizabeth picked at the imperfections in the blanket. "Nursing draws me to people. Usually I like helping them, but now I feel numb. I'm so busy battling fear that the gray inside my head never seems to clear, and today there is nothing positive to focus on." She tossed a bit of lint into the air. "I'm tired of gloom. I want to be happy again. And that brings me right here, spending time with you, Hope. You're the brightest spot in my day. Lying prostrate on the blanket, she wept bitterly. "I'm broken. And I don't know how to fix myself."

Minutes later, Elizabeth sat up and wiped her eyes on her sleeves. "Maybe Jen's right. Maybe I need to move. You know. Get a fresh start." She struggled to stand then glanced at her watch. "I've got to go," she said, shaking out the blanket and jamming it back into her bag.

"I'll be back tomorrow." She sniffled and then whispered, "I love you, Hope."

Chapter 14

The next morning, Elizabeth stood, staring at the stained brown carpet in the hallway, listening to the shuffling inside as Mrs. Krebbson made her way to her apartment door. "Hi, Mrs. Krebbson," she said to the slightly ajar door. "It's me Elizabeth."

"Lizabeth? Oh good. Glad yer back."

"I was wondering if there was any news on an evaluation. But how are you today?" Elizabeth leaned toward the crack in the door to try to get a clearer picture of her neighbor's health.

"I guess I'm okay," she said, her speech slurred.

"You are? Have you taken your medication?"

"Just those new pills Rita sent with the delivery man. Oh, and them blood pressure ones too."

"Rita sent some new ones, huh? Do you know what they're called?"

"Nope, the guy said they were ta keep me calm. Somethin' bout keepin' my heart happy."

"Your heart happy?"

"Yup."

"Mrs. Krebbson, I'm concerned that you may lose your balance. Are you okay? Shall I call for an ambulance and get you some help?"

"No! I'm not goin' anywheres. Those pills just make me sleepy. I'm okay. I appreciate your concern, but I'm gonna go lie down fer a spell."

"Okay, but what about your evaluation? Did you set up an appointment yet?"

"The delivery guy said the nurse lady would be callin' me in a couple days." Mrs. Krebbson gave Elizabeth a short wave, mumbled, "Good night," and closed the door.

Man. Now what? Elizabeth listened until the shuffling faded. *Well, she didn't fall. But she didn't even know it was morning. Time to talk to Harnold.*

Elizabeth hustled down the stairs to the basement and knocked at the office door. With no answer, she read the wall plate and quickly punched Harnold's number into her cell phone.

"Hello, Harnold. This is Elizabeth Barclay. I was checking in on Mrs. Krebbson, and she seems quite loopy. She said she received a delivery of a new medication, and I'm hoping you might have seen who made the delivery. And please let me know if you've heard anything about another evaluation. I'm really concerned. Call me back as soon as you can. Thanks."

Elizabeth turned and looked up the stairwell. *What can I do now?*

*****

Later that same afternoon at the cemetery, Elizabeth hunched down, reached into her satchel, and withdrew a small metal sign just about the width of her hand. "I had this made for you," she said to the grave. She leaned forward and pushed the spike down into the earth. "It's a name plate. Just for you." She sat back and admired the plaque with its rose-colored border. The name "Hope" was impressed into the metal and outlined in dark silver. "Oh, it's perfect! And it has a weatherproof coating, so it'll never rust."

Elizabeth placed a small pot with pink rose buds next to the sign. "I'll ask Mr. Greyson if I can plant these. It'll be extra work keeping it pruned, but it's so pretty. They are baby roses. I just had to get them." She sighed and leaned back. "I was upset the last time I was here, but I've done a lot of thinking. I am making a change. I'm looking for another job. But I'm *not* moving. I'm staying here, close to you."

Elizabeth stood and stretched. "I don't want to leave the hospital, but my long-term goals are shot now. Ya know, Wells is still doing oversight on me, even up in Cardio. I hate it. I've got to find something else." She swept her hair out from under her collar. "I've been trying to figure out what's causing all this anxiety. For a minute, I wondered if it was my mother. She drives me crazy. Well, she drives *everyone* crazy. She's hard to please, but that made me tougher. Stronger. So I'm ruling her out." She stared off into the field, remembering a reflection of her own teary-eyed teenaged face in a mirror.

"Miss Elizabeth," a deep voice called out.

Elizabeth's nerves made her whole-body jerk. "Aah!" she shrieked, grabbing her chest.

"I'm sorry. I didn't mean to scare you." Mr. Greyson peered over the hedge. "I just wanted to say hello."

"It's okay." She smiled and brushed off her jogging pants. "I'm just in my own little world, I guess," she said, as much for his benefit as for her own.

He squeezed through the hedge line and joined her. "I wanted you to know that the radar scan indicated that the grave is right where we knew it'd be."

"Oh, that's wonderful! That means they won't move her, right?"

"As far as I know she'll be staying right here. Oh, look at that," he said, eyeing the sign. "Hope. You gave her a name."

"Yes, I did." Elizabeth smiled. "This little one has given me purpose, and I'm going to see that she isn't abandoned ever again."

"I like it. It's a good name." He smiled back.

"Well, she has made me hopeful. So her name is a perfect fit." Elizabeth followed the man's gaze to the potted rose bush at her feet. "Oh, I wondered if I'd be allowed to plant this here."

"Those are pretty. They look awfully nice right there now, don't they? The management hasn't allowed them in the past, but I'll be happy to check. They might make an exception. And it can't hurt to ask now, can it?" He scratched the back of his ear. "Discovering this little one has helped you to find hope, has she?"

"Yeah. I've been struggling at work. And in finding her, I can see that hiding things can injure innocent people. I mean, someone hid *her* in this back field, and now no one knows anything about her family. And I know that I haven't been honest at work about the anxiety I'm having. I don't know exactly what has a hold on me, but whatever it is, it's a tight grip. I can't ignore it anymore. Does that even make sense?" Elizabeth eyed the headstone.

"It makes sense to me."

The two walked toward the roadway.

"Sometimes secrets are good to keep," the man said, "but other times they can harm those we care about."

"I think that says it better."

Mr. Greyson winked at Elizabeth. "You've reminded me of a story. Do you have time to hear it?"

"I have a very relaxed day planned today. I actually like your stories a lot. They make me think."

"Good. This is one that helped me." He chuckled. "A man was driving behind an old pick-up truck on the highway. It was pretty banged up, no tailgate, and it was piled high with old cast-off items: broken chairs, old metal bed springs, and items of that sort. The pile was heaped so high, the driver couldn't see out the back window. Every so often something would fall off. The drivers behind the truck would have to swerve to avoid a collision. Finally, one brave driver moved to pass the old truck. He pulled alongside and motioned to the man about the hazard, but the old driver didn't understand. He kept driving. Eventually a bucket of bolts tumbled off, and the car following him drove right over it." Mr. Greyson cleared his throat.

"Is that the end of the story? What happened to the truck driver? Did he ever stop?"

That's as far as this story goes," he replied.

"I'm sorry, Mr. Greyson, but I really don't care for this story. And I can't see how it could have helped you."

"An unfinished story doesn't settle well, does it? But it was this story that got me to thinking, wondering what if the garbage in my life was a hazard to others? Wouldn't I want to know so I could stop and secure my load?"

"Well, I would think so," Elizabeth replied.

"Of course, I would. Problems that aren't dealt with can rise up and sideline me or, worse yet, hurt someone else. No one would ever know that my load is heavy unless my actions affected them. The past is important, Miss Elizabeth. It influences us and reveals why we feel strongly about things, and it impacts how we live today."

Elizabeth walked around a rut in the road. "Okay. I know avoiding people or certain situations won't resolve my issues, but it sure makes things easier in the moment. And it gives me space to think things through. You know, when I'm frustrated I really do plan to look later at the situations that irritated me, but I think it's easier to just let them go."

"I'm sure it feels that way." He hooked his arm under hers and guided her around another pothole.

"Sometimes I just want to get through my day. I don't want to think about my *junk* or whether it has affected anyone else, you know? Sort of like I ignore the infraction and try to do better next time." She sighed.

Mr. Greyson pointed at a bird on the lawn in a tug of war with a worm. "Look at that poor worm. He woke up and peeked out of his hole, but his timing couldn't have been worse. That bird was waiting for breakfast. What's good for the bird often isn't what's best for the worm. People struggling with decisions are yanked in many directions. I'd say the first step of the equation is figuring out the issue. The second step is factoring how it affects others. The junk story raises this important question: If my baggage causes someone else to crash, do I just keep driving?" He gave Elizabeth a quick smile. "I'd like to think that I'd stop to help fix the problem or at least to apologize."

Elizabeth walked in silence, in deep thought.

"Miss Elizabeth, it seems to me that something has derailed you. The question is this: Is it your debris or someone else's that stopped you in your journey?"

She halted and faced the man. "Mr. Greyson, I have two things I'm working through, if you care to listen."

"Well, of course, I certainly do care." He stopped and gave her an understanding, kind look.

"You know, I came here specially to find you today, but I decided to visit Hope when you weren't around."

"Oh really? I would be happy to give you my cell number if you'd take it."

"Thank you. I'd really like to have it. That'd be wonderful."

"Okay, remind me before you leave. Now what's on your mind?"

"Well, there's an elderly woman, Mrs. Krebbson, in my apartment building. A few days ago, I came down on her floor and found a man trying to push his way into her place."

Mr. Greyson's eyes grew wide.

"Oh, I stopped him, but I also discovered that she has a medical condition, and the medical personnel want to move her into a senior center."

"That's a big transition. How's she handling it?"

"Not very well. She's fighting mad, but with the symptoms she's having, I think a move could be in her best interest."

"Okay, help me to understand. If it's a good move for her, then what is it that's bothering you?"

"I'm angry that, and I'm assuming it was the nursing home, sent an insensitive jerk to do her evaluation and that they want to move her without allowing her to prepare herself emotionally."

"If her health is in danger, then perhaps they need to move quickly?"

"No…well… I'm not making myself clear. There's a little more to it." She shifted from one foot to another. "I'm not explaining it well."

"You just slow down." He touched her arm and pointed at a bench under a towering maple tree. "Why don't we sit in the shade, and you can explain it again."

They walked to the bench and sat. Elizabeth took her time to get settled then, trying hard to suppress a look of despair, looked at Mr. Greyson. "You know how strongly I feel about Hope's grave being all alone in that field."

"Yes. Yes, I do."

"It's the same with my friend. She's lived alone in her apartment for years. She never goes out. And as long as I've known her, she's only talked to me through her partially opened door. She's probably agoraphobic. A sudden change like this, moving her to a place full of strangers… well, I think she'll be overwhelmed." Elizabeth's eyes flooded with tears.

"Yes, now I see."

"If that man who tried to strong-arm his way into her apartment represents the kind of people at the nursing home, I… I just don't know what to do. I can't see her living at a place that would disregard her feelings like that."

"You have a good heart, and you are a good friend to her. She's lucky to have you. I'm sure you'll both figure something out."

"I had planned on being at her evaluation to keep her from being railroaded. She's a pistol, though. You should have heard her yelling at that man in the hallway. I had a hard time believing it was the same woman who never fully opens her door." She sighed and almost in a whisper said, "I just think she needs transition time before a move happens."

"Well, at this meeting, if you say exactly what you just told me, you'll have a good chance of getting her the time she needs. I know with you there she'll be fully informed."

"Today I stopped at her door to check in, and I found her pretty wobbly from some new medication. It seems suspicious, and I'm not sure she'll let me inside to check on her. If she falls or passes out, who's going to know?"

"Does someone in the building have a copy of the key?"

"Well, I don't think she'd have shared it with anyone, but I did leave a message for the building's super. He usually brings her deliveries and watches out for her. But he wasn't in today, and he hasn't called me back."

"I can see where that would cause concern. If he doesn't get back to you, you might have to consider calling the authorities. They'd be able to get someone inside, especially if she's at risk."

"I know. I've been kicking that around, but with her agoraphobia I just didn't want to jeopardize her health further and push her over the edge emotionally."

"I can see your predicament. Perhaps you should decide after you check on her again."

"That's what I'll do. The new medication could have just kicked in as I arrived. I was really hoping Harnold could help get an eye on her, though."

"Harnold?"

"The super."

"Ah."

"Mr. Greyson, would you have any contacts with the local nursing facilities?"

"Some of my friends have undergone rehabilitation after surgery. I can make some calls and see if they have any recommendations."

"Oh, thank you. The hospital refers patients, but we don't get feedback on which facilities are good, only the ones to avoid. Any information you find would be very helpful. If she has to move, I want to make sure it's a nice place."

"Of course. I'm glad to be of assistance."

"I feel better already. I truly appreciate you."

He smiled. "Now what's this other thing you're working through?"

Elizabeth shifted on the bench. “I’ve decided I’m going to change jobs. I know I over-analyze everything, but I can’t figure out what I should do next.”

“Is hospital work too much for you right now?”

“Yes. And I’m not happy with the shift to the new department. I need to find something that’s not quite so stressful.”

“It sounds like you need some wisdom and peace.”

“For sure.”

He touched her arm. “You are wonderful with people. I know you’ll find another avenue for using your nurturing skills. I’ll be praying for you.”

“Thanks. Just having you to talk to makes me feel better. I don’t think you know just how special you are, Mr. Greyson.” Elizabeth patted his hand.

He opened his arms wide, and she allowed him to give her a gentle hug.

“Thank *you*, Miss Elizabeth,” he said with a catch in his voice. “I’ve often imagined how hugging Kennedy would feel if she had been given the time to grow up. You’re a real blessing to me.” He released her and pulled a hanky and rolled-up newspaper from his back pocket. Tucking the paper under his arm, he wiped his eyes with his hanky.

"You must miss her very much," Elizabeth said.

"Oh, I do. I do. I miss my Marie too. I feel her with me most every day while I'm working. And I get to visit both graves daily. I know they're not really here, but it's good to see their names and to be able to care for them this way. I designed their headstone right after their funeral. It was my last act of love for them." He blew his nose and whispered, "Excuse me," and placed the hanky back in his pocket.

"Oh, but it seems to me that caring for their graves is an act of love too."

"That it is," he replied. Taking a deep breath, he opened the newspaper. "Now, there's something in here I want to show you." Pointing to a small column, he handed the newspaper to her.

Elizabeth quickly scanned the page, focusing on a short article about an unknown grave in this very cemetery. "It's about Hope!"

"Yes. A reporter came to the office asking about a misplaced grave. Apparently a courthouse employee gave her the lead. I think your calling around trying to discover something about the baby's family tipped them off."

Elizabeth stared intently at the paper without responding.

"You can keep the newspaper. The article covers the cemetery's history, and it mentions that you are caring for the grave."

"Me? Oh dear. Perhaps Hope's real story will come to light after all. Someone must have a clue as to how she ended up back there." Elizabeth pointed in the grave's direction. "But it doesn't matter anymore, not to me. In *my* heart she'll always be my Hope."

"I believe that," Mr. Greyson said with a smile.

Chapter 15

The next morning, Elizabeth looked up and smiled, a cool, gentle breeze caressed her bare arms. It was as if spring were celebrating in a complete array of vibrant greens, fragrant flowers blossomed, and birds lilted their serenade overhead.

Oakwood Cemetery had few early morning visitors. Two women, possibly sisters in their sixties, stood in front of a large, pink-toned marker near the front gate. As Elizabeth jogged by the women, she read the name on the headstone: Tysell, Madeline, 1933-1979. *She died young. Maybe she was their mother.* Elizabeth slowed her steps and looked closer at the pair wearing similar clothing. *Definitely sisters. Stop being nosy, Elizabeth!*

Picking up her pace toward the little grave, the now familiar headstones along the way greeted her, and she greeted them back. "Good morning, Mr. Graham, Mother Bisnett, and Graham Jr." *The cemetery seems so friendly. It must be my mood.*

Elizabeth's cell phone rang and she stopped, fumbling in her jeans pocket to retrieve it. She looked at the phone and noticed her sister's name. *Gotta love Caller ID.* "Hi, Jen. Can you still make lunch today?"

"Nope, change of plans. They bumped up a closing to tomorrow, and I already have another one scheduled. I'll need the full morning to get all the paperwork together, but I do have a few minutes now. Can you chat?"

"I can talk, but I'd rather have lunch with you."

"Me too. So, what happened yesterday at the hospital? Did you meet with the administrator? What about getting the reference you needed from Wells?"

"I didn't have to deal with her at all. I met with Director Carlyle."

"Woo-hoo!" Jen squealed.

"And he gave me a glowing report with one caveat—my avoidance of certain patients," Elizabeth said softly.

"What does that mean?"

"Apparently, Wells' report stated that I avoid working with pregnant women. And that any future nursing position should be informed of that."

"What?!" her sister said. "That's ridiculous. Can they do that?"

"I guess. I can't believe she wrote that, though."

"I'm confused. Where did she come up with something like that?"

"My anxiety attack happened while I was treating a pregnant patient. Apparently that was Wells' conclusion. But I've treated pregnant patients for years. What a crock! I never avoid my patients. Oh, and Director Carlyle also wished me good luck on my new—"

"You're at the cemetery again, aren't you?" Jen asked with a note of annoyance.

Elizabeth adjusted her shoulder bag and answered slowly, "Y-yes."

"You're there an awful lot, Bitty. I don't think it's healthy walking among the dead. Are you sure you're okay?"

"Don't start with me, Jen. You know I've got a lot going on. I'm trying to figure out my meltdown, so it doesn't happen again. It's quiet, and I can think better here." Then with a snap, Elizabeth said, "I'm fine, and walking is healthy."

Silence on the other end of the phone.

Elizabeth continued bluntly. "Jen, you're about the only person I talk to ... ever. I know we've discussed my need to make new friends." Elizabeth kicked at a stone on the path. "I agree, but I think I've forgotten how."

"I'm glad you brought that up because I've been thinking too. What about old friends? How about connecting with some friends from college? Do you keep in touch with any of them?"

"No."

"What about Molly? She was in all your nursing classes. You should try connecting with her. Look her up on the internet."

"It's been too long. We haven't talked since I left Cedar Point."

"Okay, but I do think looking up old friends is a good idea. All you have to do is just send a quick text.

Something like, 'Wow, glad to find you,' is all it takes. Just think about it. Okay?"

Elizabeth paused, then said, "I'm thinking about dating again."

"What? That's huge! That's even better. A boyfriend will get you out of the house, and he'll have a few friends you might like. Who's the guy? Do I know him?"

"His name is Dr. Whitman."

"A doctor from the hospital? Tell me more."

"His first name is Reggie."

"I'm so glad for you, Bitts! I don't think you've dated since high school."

"Nope. Too busy."

"Whatever happened with David? Do you hear from him at all?"

Elizabeth didn't respond.

Jen said, "Wanna tell me about your doctor friend?"

"Not yet. Just that he's asked me out, and I like him."

"Why aren't you dating him already?"

"Anxiety. I just need to think things through. You keep pushing me. Telling me to get out more. So I thought I'd let you know that I *am* working on it."

"If you're not going to tell me more about your doctor, what about this new job? Are you nervous? When do you start?"

"I'm not too nervous about it. I start next week. The first few days are going to be hard. It's at a nursing home. Just learning my way around the place and meeting all the residents will be the toughest. I'm working alongside my supervisor for the first week. That'll make me a little jittery, you know, but I'm excited too."

"So, what will you be doing?"

"Evaluations, blood pressure checks, medication disbursement, and monitoring exercise class for starters. I think this will be a good change." She took a swipe at a bug and then added through clenched teeth, "And there shouldn't be any pregnant women to avoid."

"I still can't believe she wrote that," Jen said.

"Yeah, I'm still processing it."

"Well, after having worked in the ER, I hope this new job isn't too boring for you."

"I'll know that soon enough. Developing relationships with the residents will be a positive change for me. You never said that my new friends had to be *my* age. I'll have a whole new sphere of people to choose from." Elizabeth laughed, and Jen joined in.

Elizabeth continued. "I don't know why I always felt like I had to compete with my peers. I'm sure that's why I'm virtually friendless, except for you … and Mr. Greyson."

"Is that the old caretaker?"

"Yeah. I like him a lot. He's a good listener, and he's pretty profound."

"Well, at least, you have someone to talk to. And I'm excited about Dr. Reggie. You will have to tell me more, but I gotta go. I'll call you back tonight." Jen hung up without a goodbye.

Elizabeth shook her head. "Goodbye," she said to her silent phone. Looking ahead, she eyed the path veering to the right that boasted two large oak trees with intertwined branches arched over a small ravine. To the right of the pathway, a trickling creek gurgled a welcoming tune. *How beautiful. I can't believe this cemetery with all its beauty is in the center of town.*

When she arrived at Hope's grave, Elizabeth beamed with delight. The new sign that she had placed there glistened in the sunlight next to the pink roses.

"It looks awesome!" Elizabeth said to the grave. "Good morning, baby girl." Pulling a small blanket out of her satchel, Elizabeth spread out the blanket and relaxed on it. "Soon I'll only be able to visit after work. I was worried that I wouldn't get a recommendation, but it's all good." *Except the pregnant women portion of the review.* Elizabeth stretched out her legs and thought back to Jen's question about David and their break up. *Go away, David.*

She caressed her feet and let her body rest in a folded position, willing her mind to be silent. A teenage girl's face emerged from the past. It was the same face she had remembered before. *Who was she?*

"Great. Now I'm dwelling on an old break-up when all I want to do is look forward." *New job, Elizabeth, focus.* "Wait—Mr. Greyson's junk story. I should try to process this." Another image came to mind as she sat upright. "Hope, I remember that girl now. I passed her entering a medical office. She was crying as she left the building. She seemed so small. You know, I could sense her distress. I could see the pain on her face. But as soon as I entered the office, the girl, the rest of the world, slipped away. I remember how embarrassed I was to be there. I was sure that everyone knew something intimate about me. Oh yeah, and the number thirty-six. That's how many floor tiles there were in the waiting room." Elizabeth gave half a chuckle, "Three of them were cracked. You know, that girl's face was the last image I had when I went in… went in to… to have an abortion."

Tears flooded Elizabeth's eyes, and she cried bitterly from deep inside as locked-up memories escaped from the recesses of her mind. Her cry rang out, echoing through the empty field as she lay face down on the grave and sobbed. Years of repressed affliction oozed out, watering the soil. The anguish of unspoken heartbreak, of hidden things, of the dying of hopes and dreams, it all poured out in a rush of deep emotion. When words finally surfaced, she mumbled into the blanket. “I… can’t… believe… I… did that.” She inhaled a deep breath and continued. “I’m so, so sorry. Don’t think bad of me, Hope. Please don’t hate me. I love you so much!”

Elizabeth closed her eyes and remembered the day she told David, “It’s okay, I can do my classes and have the baby too. I know I can. I’ll finish up online after the baby arrives.”

She moved to embrace him, but he stepped aside, barely placing a hand on her shoulder. “We’re not ready to be parents, Beth. I can’t support a family. Not without an education.”

“You’ll still get to go to college.” Elizabeth touched the hand on her shoulder willing him to take hers. “We talked about having children. This one is just coming a little sooner than we expected.”

He shook his head. “No. This is not the time. I’m not ready to be a father. Not yet. Marriage was going to be *after* graduation. And babies come after we live a little. That’s the plan. But a kid now? Well— this *is not* a part of the plan, Elizabeth.” His face fiery red, he stared at her, backed away, and sneered, "You planned this, didn't you?"

"What? No, David!"

"This is not happening," he said. "I'm not attending college with a pregnant girlfriend. Nope. Not happening. This is on you. You did this. You take care of it, Elizabeth. You're on your own!"

As she lay on the grave, Elizabeth jumped when she felt something on her hand. She sat up and brushed a small spider off. Then she focused on the grave. "I couldn't tell my parents, Hope. I just couldn't. So, I went to the clinic. I don't remember how I finished those last weeks of school." She pulled a tissue out of her bag and wiped away the barrage of tears. "Why did I let fear win? Oh, what I would give to have that child now." She choked on her words, "If only—" Again she lay on Hope's grave, weeping, releasing unimaginably deep, heart-gripping pain until a restless sleep overtook her.

Chapter 16

The next morning, Elizabeth sat at a booth in Cinny's Coffee and Bagel Shop and watched out the window as Jenny headed toward the shop. When Jenny spotted Elizabeth, she waved then, upon entering, snagged a waitress before she got to the booth. "Have you ordered yet?" Jenny asked. "I just did."

Elizabeth didn't respond.

Jen slid into the booth and placed her handbag on the faux leather seat. She looked at Elizabeth expectantly. "Well?"

"I'm just waiting for you to get settled. Good morning."

Folding her hands on the table, Jen said, "It's been a crazy one! I've already been to the office, and the closing paperwork for Brown Street is being copied in triplicate as we eat. It's that pretty little blue Cape Cod home over near the dog groomer's business. You know which one it is. So have you ordered?"

Elizabeth chuckled. "You're too much! Yes, I've ordered. Here comes our coffee."

The waitress placed a French press coffee pot and a cup in front of Jen while Elizabeth received a tall mug of hot coffee.

"Thank you," the sisters said in unison.

"So tell me about all this outdoor walking you've been doing. What's up with that?" Jen gave a slow press on the handle, watching the liquid pass through the sieve.

"We already discussed this. It's just a quiet place to think."

"You're on your feet all day at work. I can't believe you want to walk more. What happened to thinking at home?" Jen poured coffee into her cup and added cream.

"What's wrong with walking?" Elizabeth answered. "I can't believe that I've found a beautiful, safe place to think, and you have a problem with it. Exercise is healthy, remember?" She sipped her coffee as the waitress brought their meals.

"Ooh," Jen said, "your bagel looks good, but the croissants here are the best."

"If you eat too many of those, *you'll* have to walk to erase all those calories."

"Bagels aren't calorie-free either." Jen nibbled on her croissant.

"Let's catch up on the good stuff. Tell me about your boss. Did he hire any extra help? And how can papers be copied in triplicate while you eat here with me? I want details."

"No one is permanently hired, but my friend Rena is helping," Jen said between bites. "She's in real estate and knows the basics. My boss, Mr. Jamison, is only willing to pay her per diem. It's enough help to get a little time off for an occasional coffee break with you."

"And I'm thrilled. Thank her for me, would you?"

She sighed. "Well, all this work isn't doing much for my love life. Trent and I have only had a couple of lunches together, and both times we ate at the office. We've been to one movie and our theater date. There's another movie we'd like to see after my boss gets back from this next trip. Honestly, I'm so exhausted at the end of the day, right now I don't think I could stay awake through an entire movie." Jen lifted her cup and blew across the surface.

"You're even busier than I was at the hospital. I'm glad Rena's helping you. You know, your immune system will get compromised if you don't get enough rest."

"Yup, and this is coming from my workhorse sister." Jen took a quick sip, set her cup down, and leaned forward. "Okay, now give. Tell me all about your doctor!"

Cradling her mug, Elizabeth smiled. "Now that's a subject change."

"Just spill. I've only got an hour."

"Okay. Here's the quick version. We worked together in the ER. We shared some lunch breaks, and he asked me out. And I think I'm finally ready to say yes."

"Awesome. And you never mentioned him because?"

"Because … I wasn't sure what was triggering my panic. So I put him off."

Jen just stared.

"I didn't think it would be fair to start a relationship." Elizabeth's eyes moistened, and she grabbed a napkin and dabbed her eyes. "Basically, because I'm such a mess."

Jen reached across the table and patted her sister's arm. "I never saw you as a mess. You're someone I love, and sometimes you struggle."

"My anxiety is unpredictable. Did you know that today I stood around the corner for about three minutes just to get my nerve up to come inside here? Shaky hands, sweaty palms, and my heart was racing. I am a mess."

"What? Today? I didn't know that—"

"I'm fine now. I had calmed down before I even came in, but I never know when it's going to hit or how severe it's going to be. I tiptoe through my day, self-evaluating every encounter. I had a panic attack at work, and when you weren't available I had no one else to talk to."

"I'm sorry. Have you considered talking to someone… you know, a professional to discuss things?"

"You mean a therapist?"

Jen nodded, and Elizabeth pulled her hand away. "You've mentioned that before. And, yeah, I've thought about it. But it's hard to hide something like that from the medical community. I was worried about losing my job, but that's not an issue anymore. Do you know that they have ratings and reviews for therapists online now? See, I *am* thinking about it." Elizabeth took another sip of coffee and signaled the waitress for a take-out container. "I know you think it's weird that I spend so much time in the cemetery, but I'd like you to come see it with me."

"Well, ah—"

"You said you're not on the clock until nine today. Please take a ride with me. I'll have you back in plenty of time."

"Well—"

"Jen, we can take our coffee with us. Please?"

*****

Elizabeth parked along the grass about halfway to the back of the cemetery. The sisters walked side by side, coffee cups in hand.

"Just check out this stream," Elizabeth said. "Don't you love how the branches seem to hang over it?"

Jen smiled. "Yeah, and I just love the smell of the fresh-cut grass."

"Mr. Greyson is out here every day mowing, trimming branches, and just keeping things neat."

"Tell me about him, Bitts. You said he's old."

"I think he's got to be in his seventies. He doesn't seem old to me. He's worked here for fifteen years. Come over here." Elizabeth pointed to her left. "See that headstone there?"

"Greyson, that's his name. Is that—"

"He lost his wife and daughter in a fire years ago. That's how he came to work here."

"How awful."

"It is, but he says he's happy to be watching over their markers."

"I see."

As they walked on the road, Elizabeth asked, "Jen, do you ever think about visiting Dad's grave?"

"Ugh, no Bitts. I don't like cemeteries."

"I never did either until I started coming here. I've been thinking, I'd like to see how Dad's grave looks, and I want to bring him flowers."

Jen gave her a weak smile.

"Look, here's what I really wanted you to see." Elizabeth pulled Jen onto the grass and behind the row of hedges.

"I know. This must be the famous baby grave."

"Hidden but relevant." Elizabeth pointed. "She's right there."

"Oh, she has a little name marker and flowers." Jen stopped and stared at her sister. "You did this?"

Elizabeth nodded. "I've been clearing off the weeds and making her plot nice."

"I see, but we talked about this. Why not let the cemetery workers do that? Your friend, the caretaker? It's his job. Isn't it?"

"At first, I wasn't sure why I was drawn to the grave—drawn to her. She was simply an abandoned baby. Perhaps I was trying to right a wrong. But snippets of my past have been creeping back. I think I figured out why it's been so important to me."

"Oka-a-a-y."

"This is hard to share, but—" Elizabeth wrung her free hand and then rubbed it on her trembling legs.

Jen touched her arm. "Just say it. We're adults. Is this about Mom and camping?"

"No. It's just that I've never told anyone. I … I had an abortion."

Jen's silence was deafening.

"Did you hear me, Jen?"

"Yes." After a long pause, Jen said, "So this wasn't recent?"

"No, back in high school. With David."

"David? Why didn't you say something? We lived in the same house. You could have told me."

"You were fifteen, and as I remember, you were kind of a brat." Elizabeth bumped her sister's shoulder then stared at the nameplate. "I didn't tell *anyone*. It was a few weeks before graduation. College was so close. David wasn't ready—" Pausing with near panic, she felt her fingernails digging into her palms. "I didn't talk about it. I didn't think about it. Well, not much. I just did it." Tears slid down her cheeks.

Jen touched her arm. “I wish you had said something.”

“I was too self-focused at the time. Busy with work and school.”

Jen looked away and shook her head. “I’m not sure how I would have handled it at that time anyway, so it was probably a good call.”

“You looked up to me since I was your big sis. At least, I think you did. And I sure didn’t want Mom finding out.”

“I wouldn’t have said anything to her.”

“I know.” Elizabeth pointed to the headstone. “So, when I found this little grave, I was drawn to it. I felt awful that a baby was abandoned out here all alone. Then yesterday all those old memories came flooding back. You know, back then for just a few weeks of my life, I thought about being a mom. I wondered if it would be a boy or a girl and if the baby would look like me. After the abortion everything was a blur. I just threw myself into finals, I guess. I couldn’t let people in. I saw what happened to other girls. If my friends had known about it, they would have judged me bigtime. I guess I just buried the memories. All this time ...."

Elizabeth looked at her sister, surprised to see tears flooding Jen's eyes. Elizabeth pulled her into an embrace and in a broken voice said, "I'm sorry, Jen. I never considered how you'd feel having lost the opportunity to be an aunt. Are you okay?"

"I wish you would have talked to me about this before, Bitts. We could have helped each other through it."

"What...what do you mean?"

"I had an abortion two years ago."

Elizabeth's mouth dropped open. "What? But weren't you and Will married then?"

"We'd only been married a few months, and we were saving for a house. Will said it was bad timing. So I had an abortion."

"Oh, Jen, I'm so sorry."

Embracing her sister, Elizabeth asked, "Was it your decision?"

"Pretty much. We discussed it. I understood Will's perspective. But I really missed Dad, and I thought having a baby would be great. It's not like we were trying—" Jen turned away. "I don't think I was ready to be a mom, but afterwards it was the little things that got to me. And I couldn't forget the sound of that stupid suction machine they used." Jen was crying now. "Will and I started arguing more, and we couldn't make things work."

"He still loves you; you know."

Jen pulled from Elizabeth's embrace and turned away, still teary. "Probably. But it's over. I'm not going back to Cedar Point."

"Have you spoken with anyone about your abortion?"

"A few friends know about it. And I talked to a counselor before taking the job here. I'm not as flighty as you may think."

"I never said you were flighty."

"I know." Jen turned back to her sister. "But you are always talking so highly about Will. I know our being separated bothers you."

"I think Will filled in some of the emptiness I felt after losing Dad. I liked having a guy around again. I thought you picked a mate very well. Much better than I did."

"Man, I wish we had talked about this sooner."

"Hey, I worked hard to keep my motto alive: 'Leave the past out of the present, and keep the present carefully concealed.'"

"Well, you are a stickler for rules. I wonder who you take after."

"Jen, don't start!"

"I kind of understand why you spend so much time here. It's not the creepy place I imagined it was," Jen said with a half-smile.

"Actually, it's quite lovely. Did you notice all the flowers? And wait until you meet Mr. Greyson."

"You win. I'll stop bugging you about coming here."

"And maybe you'll join me on a walk sometime?"

"Perhaps. But what I need right now is a ride to my office." Jen released a sweet smile.

"Yikes! I forgot. Let's go!"

Chapter 17

On Monday morning, Mr. Greyson abandoned his lawn tractor and joined Elizabeth on her morning trek. "Good morning. It's another beautiful day."

"Yes, it is." She slowed down and leaned against a towering elm tree to catch her breath.

"You're a bit later in your walk today."

"I am. I'm feeling relaxed and free this morning. It's wonderful."

"May I say that you look like glowing sunshine? And it seems to me like slowing down has worked well for you. I'm glad to see it. Did you notice that the cemetery's a bit busier this morning?"

She stepped away from a spider crawling on the tree trunk, and brushed off her shoulder with a shiver then turned her attention to Mr. Greyson. "Busier as in more burials?"

"No. We've more visitors than we normally have. I think that newspaper article sparked some interest."

"It's funny that you say that because on my last day at the hospital, several coworkers were discussing it.

They had a lot questions." Elizabeth looked the man straight in the eyes, and joked, "I felt most popular."

He laughed. "Good. Let's go see the grave together." They began walking toward it. "You know, with all the interest in the baby, our office ran out of maps. Linda's been marking the new ones with the location of the little grave.

"On the cemetery map? Oh my. Everyone can find her then."

"Yes, and it's satisfying. It's been a long time since that part of the cemetery has seen such attention."

As they passed four cars lining the road, Elizabeth spotted in the distance several people milling about Hope's plot, laughing and chatting with one another.

"I think it's too busy for me to visit today." *Sorry, baby girl. I guess I have to share you now.*

"Oh," Mr. Greyson said as he and Elizabeth stopped at the roadside. "Does that bother you to see people visiting the grave?"

"Not really," Elizabeth said, although she wasn't quite sure it was the truth.

"She's getting a lot of attention." Mr. Greyson pulled a plastic bag from his pocket, unfolded it, and stooped to pick up some litter.

"You are always working," Elizabeth said, her tone complimentary.

"Oh, it just comes natural. I don't think about it. I don't even remember putting this bag in my pocket, but there always seems to be one there when I need it. Do you want to leave?"

"Yes, let's go."

As they walked away, Elizabeth suddenly stopped. "Mr. Greyson, how do people move on after a loss?"

"You know, I was just thinking about my Marie." His eyes sparkled as he looked off into the distant trees. "Give me a minute." He pulled out a hanky from his back pocket and blew his nose. "I was lost for a good long while. I mean, I was lost in my thoughts. When the fog lifted, I guess I simply trusted that, like most things in life, my pain would be something I'd learn from."

As the man stared into the distance, Elizabeth began reading the headstones nearby to allow him the space he needed. Staring at what looked like another child's grave, she studied a pair of cherubs and small heart etchings on the marker. *Perhaps angels are watching over new charges now like they once did these people.*

As a few cars crawled past in the direction of Hope's grave. Elizabeth turned toward it. *I'll come tomorrow, baby girl, before the crowd arrives.*

Just as Elizabeth turned toward Mr. Greyson, he said, "How did I move on? I trusted … trusted that my loved ones were in a better place. Every day I made the choice to live. I forced myself to get up and to go places. I deliberately pasted on a smile until one day my smile was real again."

"It sounds so difficult. Does it still hurt?" Elizabeth shifted her attention from Mr. Greyson toward two new groups of people walking toward Hope's grave.

"The pain isn't the same. I admit at times I keenly felt their loss, but over the years, the hurt has changed to sadness at not being able to hold them, but I'd not wish them back. Where they are now is pain-free. And someday I'll see them again."

"What I don't understand is why *do* people have to suffer? Why pain? Why can't life be just filled with good things?"

"There's not a person alive that wouldn't have a tough time navigating that question. I can only share with you what I've learned. No one likes to struggle or hurt. But hard situations challenge us to think deep. It prompts us to move to new places. This burial ground is a reminder that we all come with an expiration date. Unfortunately, some endings come sooner than we're prepared for." He paused as Elizabeth dabbed her tears. "My sadness eased as I focused on being grateful for the gift that my family was to me. I think my grief could've turned into anger, and then I'd be a mighty bitter person. And my Marie. She was one special gift. She wouldn't want me to live in anger and bitterness." He sighed. "I guess I don't have an exact answer to the why of pain, but I know my heart is sure tender to those struggling through dark seasons."

"Are you saying that *my* struggles might be helpful some day?"

"I'm confident they will. We always learn something from hardship. Sometimes we learn what we shouldn't do, and other times our conquest is the inspiration for someone else to push through theirs."

"Yeah, you may be right."

"Once I realized that I'm not entitled to happiness, it changed my life. Now when I find something good, I embrace it. I celebrate it, and I'm grateful for it. I'm sorry to admit that I had become a most selfish person, Miss Elizabeth. I had never learned to celebrate each day as the gift that it is."

"Oh, you're the least selfish person I know." Elizabeth wiped her eyes again. "The work you do here is much more than a job to you. You watch over so many. You take time to talk with people like me. You care."

"That I do," he said, slipping his arm gently around her shoulders. "People are a priority. Tell me, young lady, how are you doing? And how did that elderly neighbor of yours make out?"

"Oh! It's amazing. At the interview for my new job, I mentioned having a neighbor looking for a placement, and it all worked out. She'll be moving in right after I start. I'm so happy for her. I'll actually be right there to help her!"

"Wonderful. See, sometimes people are the answer to prayer. That, indeed, is a very good solution." As they sauntered toward the cemetery entrance, he added, "This new job will be quite the change. How do you feel about it?"

"I'm struggling but not so much about that. I truly believe this is the best job for me, at least, for now."

"Good. I'm glad."

"I'm sure my mother will be disappointed with this change. She has such high expectations. It's not a better position. It's less money, but it'll also be less stressful."

"Well then, I'd say it's a good decision. All mommas want what is best for their children. If you've found a job that you're happy doing, I think she'll be okay with it."

"She's coming to visit me next month. She's very blunt, so I'll know exactly how she feels soon enough," she replied with a touch of sarcasm.

With a glint in his eyes, he said, "I'm glad to hear she's visiting. Please try to make the most of that relationship. Sometimes it takes asking the right question to understand people. Your mother raised a real nice young woman, so she must be a great lady herself."

"Thank you. But her personality rubs me the wrong way. It's difficult."

"It very well may be that her personality has helped to make you into the wonderful woman you are today."

"I'll admit that it has made me stronger, but I really have a way of messing things up."

"What do you mean?"

"I messed up my job. And poor Reggie. My indecisiveness really messed with his head."

"Who's Reggie?"

"Oh, he's a doctor at the hospital who'd like to date me."

"I'd say you're back on track now, though. Wouldn't you?"

She nodded slightly.

"And this situation with Hope's grave caused you to think deep, and look at what that did. It moved you to new places. Places you're supposed to be."

Elizabeth released a subtle smile.

"I'd say you're a bit more like our hero milkman, Leonard Benson, than you'd ever think."

"Oh, I'm nothing like him."

"Why, you managed to get your friend into the same nursing home where you'll be working. She'll be safe, and she won't be alone. I'd say that's a pretty creative solution."

Elizabeth smiled, averting his gaze. "Thank you for those kind words."

"Well done." Mr. Greyson laughed. "Shall we grab a glass of milk to celebrate?"

"Don't be silly. Let's leave the milk and the milk truck to Leonard. You must know that a real celebration deserves ice cream."

"See, that's another creative solution! But it's too early for ice cream. We should go some evening. I'd really like that."

"Of course. But it's *never* too early for ice cream, not for me."

As they approached the lawn mower, Mr. Greyson blurted, "Oh, I almost forgot." He lifted the mower seat and pulled out a rolled-up newspaper. Pulling out a folded piece of paper from it, he said, "I have last night's newspaper article for you. And I think this is what's drawing the crowd today. A reporter discovered a possible identity for the baby."

"Seriously?" Her voice went up an octave.

Mr. Greyson handed her the article, and she began to read. "Possible connection found to the recently discovered baby grave in Oakwood Cemetery, Aurora Springs. According to an article in 'The Hudson Express,' a prominent couple, Mr. and Mrs. Elijah Martin, were discovered dead in their wrecked 1903 Tonneau in the township of Daniville, New York. According to close friends, they were enroute to pay a ransom for their kidnapped baby. Their daughter was never found."

Elizabeth's voice weakened. "This reporter thinks that Hope was their child?"

"Yes. That reporter did some amazing detective work. Daniville is just a half-hour from here," Mr. Greyson said, then cleared his throat.

Elizabeth handed back the article.

He reached for the article but then shook his head. "No. You keep it."

Drawing the article to her chest she said, "So Hope's parents died. She wasn't abandoned. They were trying to get her back! She *was* wanted! Oh, I really had hoped that'd be her story. But how sad for them all."

"Yes, it is a strong possibility. It's a well-written article, and there's plenty of tidbits that support it. And even if it does answer who she was, it can't tell us how she came to be buried here." He had her pull a folded piece of paper he had placed inside the newspaper. "I thought you'd be most interested in this article. I found it online."

"Another article?"

"I copied it for you. My sister lives about an hour from here, and her paper ran the same story ours did about you and the baby's grave. This paper lists some responses on their opinion page. Go ahead, read it. The first comment is from my sister's neighbor."

"Why, it says that she's tending to the grave of an eighteen-month-old boy. Oh, his grave was *orphaned* too!"

"Yes, and it goes on to say … well,… she's decided to adopt his grave and care for it like you've adopted Hope's."

Elizabeth's eyes grew wide. "But why?"

"Apparently you're not the only one with a need to nurture something." Mr. Greyson rested his hands on her shoulders and gently turned her. "Look over there," he whispered.

Elizabeth surveyed a graveside across the road. A woman was kneeling with a pot of white flowers by her side. "I don't understand. What am I looking for?"

"You can't read the headstone from here, but it reads, 'Baby Son.' When I passed by earlier, the woman was singing a lullaby."

"There's another grave here with an unknown child?" Elizabeth's voice cracked.

"Yes, and another person caring for the grave. It appears to be therapeutic. The opinion piece also mentions that their local hospital had an increase in volunteers to hold their premature babies." He chuckled. "They had so many volunteers they ran out of babies."

Elizabeth stood speechless.

"I think it all comes back to what we talked about earlier, that caring for others is truly a path to healing."

"I believe it," Elizabeth said, watching the woman talking to the grave. "I know it helped me."

"Oh, and one more thing about Hope's grave. Now you're still welcome to walk the cemetery, but you should probably call before coming out for your next visit."

"Why? Am I being limited? Just because it's busy? I don't understand." She took a step back from the man and squared her shoulders.

"No, nothing like that. It just might save you a trip. A couple of our guys will be excavating out here soon. They'll be uprooting some bushes for the expansion. It'll be a busy spot for a few days with the reseeding and all. Hope's area will be blocked off until they're—"

"You've lost me. What expansion?"

"I've been asked to oversee the removal of those shrubs that block her grave. The ones everybody's been wiggling through. We're reworking the hedge line. The new bushes will go behind her grave. We're bringing her inside."

"Oh!" Elizabeth gasped.

Chapter 18

One week later, Dr. Reggie Whitman stood with folded arms under the tall oak tree near Hope's plot, allowing Elizabeth privacy with the grave.

The landscapers had moved the hedges behind the grave and added two small, angled hedge rows connected to those hedges. Hope was now in her own space inside the cemetery.

Elizabeth stood at the headstone, beaming her widest smile. *You're no longer alone, Hope!*

"Oh, look," she said to Reggie as she pointed," there's a bench back here too. How wonderful!" She read the plaque on the top board: 'In Memory of Marie and Kennedy Greyson.' *Oh Mr. Greyson. How sweet of you!* "Look, Hope. There's no need to wait for grass to grow. They used sod!"

Elizabeth carefully stepped onto the new grass near the headstone. Kneeling down, she said, "Oh, it's so soft." She touched the greenery, her fingers enjoying the silkiness of the rich rolled carpet. "This is so much nicer than those weeds. It's like a lush blanket. And no more mud! Isn't it wonderful?" She glanced back at Reggie, and blushed at his smile.

"Well Hope, I did it. I started my new job. I'm meeting all the residents. And best of all, Mrs. Krebbson will be moving there in a few days. Isn't that great? Neither one of you will be alone!"

As Elizabeth stood and stared at the headstone, tears welled in her eyes. She whispered, "I finally figured out that I've been battling myself all this time. And I never knew it. I thought stuffing my feelings into a box and hiding them away was the key to staying strong. But what can you do when the box overflows? You know, I think I'm brave enough to open it now. I need to start dealing with my issues. The days of punishing myself are over."

She reached forward and touched the headstone. "I want to learn to forgive myself, baby girl. Mr. Greyson says we all make mistakes and that true healing comes in time. I'm never going to forget that I would've been the momma of a six-year-old. I've wasted too much time hiding. No more. I've found a counselor online that will help me deal with things." She glanced at Reggie, and he smiled again. "I'm going to learn to live."

Elizabeth took a deep breath of fresh air, and noticing that Reggie and three others were approaching, she whispered, "I'm so glad I have you, Hope. Finding you has changed my world."

The End

Dear Reader,

I'm thrilled to introduce you to our wonderful Mr. Greyson and Elizabeth. Anxiety is a serious topic, and I'm a strong believer in setting aside any judgment for the benefit of healing.

I hope you enjoyed seeing Elizabeth conquer this challenging season in her life. I love that she was able to make positive life changes by rethinking how she saw herself.

Traumatizing events can overload one's system. Old, festering wounds need to be cleaned out for proper healing. (Thanks, Mr. Greyson!)

It's not easy to forgive yourself, especially when we're focused on "old junk." If you struggle with depression or anxiety, I pray you'll find a bit of hope in this story.

Elizabeth's techniques for coping with her anxiety are suggestions for Post-Traumatic Stress Disorder sufferers, but they can work for all kinds of anxiety. Check out the next section to see a list of the techniques she used.

And there's more adventure ahead, and a lot more action in the next book now that Elizabeth has moved on from the ER. And yes, Dr. Reggie is along for the ride. Hope you'll check it out and drop me a line @RedefiningDebbie.com. I love to hear from my readers. And stay connected with my newsletter. It'll get you the inside scoop and even some scenes that didn't make the book.

Again, thank you for taking this journey with Elizabeth. God bless you. I wish *you* a blessed journey ahead.

Debbie G.

Helpful techniques to battle anxiety

Sitting in a dark room
Exercise
Candles: scented oils like lavender, chamomile
Showers or soaking baths
Object focus
Deep breathing
Repeating a positive phrase
Grounding: remind yourself that you're here and you're okay. Remember Elizabeth's hair tugging?
Herbal teas
Counseling is a recommended option. Talking about your difficulties to someone who won't judge you can be life-changing. Working through forgiveness is often easier with a good listener. And consider medication if it's recommended.

Imbalances in life don't have to keep us stuck. Cheer for yourself with every step forward. You've earned it!
*Note- I'm not a medical professional, but these are techniques that have helped me and my loved ones.

Discussion Questions

Chapter 1 - Life can sometimes feel overwhelming. Elizabeth had something she repeated to block out pressing concerns. What is it that causes you to feel anxious? Is there something you recite to get through times of stress? Does it always work?

Chapter 2 - Dreams can be a way your body processes internal information. Elizabeth was frustrated when she didn't know who was crying in her dream. Are there times when you feel you can't adequately meet someone's needs? What techniques do you use to handle frustration? How do you decide what is your responsibility and what is not?

Chapter 3 - A concern for her neighbor allowed Elizabeth to bravely confront an intruder. Why do you think she didn't hesitate to do that when she's doubtful of her abilities at work? At the cemetery, Elizabeth pushed away memories from her past. Do you think this was helpful? Why/why not?

Chapter 4 - "Leave the past out of the present, and keep the present carefully concealed," was Elizabeth's motto. In what ways would this motto work well in your life? How might it be bad? Elizabeth's co-workers think she might be doing drugs. Has anyone ever accused you of doing something that you weren't doing? How did you handle it?

Chapter 5 - Elizabeth's mother had strong opinions about Jen's after-work hours. How would you rate how the mother expressed her concerns to her daughter? Is speaking to a loved one about an important issue easy or difficult for you? Can you think of a positive outcome of sharing your concerns with someone?

Chapter 6 - A monument excluding family members' names infuriated Elizabeth and sparked a memory of feeling belittled. How do you deal with hurtful comments? Why did Elizabeth disregard Mr. Greyson's compliment? What ruler do you use to measure yourself? Is it accurate?

Chapter 7 - "...your deeds are your monuments." This comment earned Mr. Greyson a hug. Elizabeth felt good about being a nurse. But not all deeds are good. Can people change their feelings about their past? About mistakes? Elizabeth was told she had made an indelible impression. Has someone made an indelible impression on you? In what way?

Chapter 8 - Elizabeth was against her sister's decision to leave her marriage. Why do you think she was so resistant? Elizabeth found it difficult to express her concerns. How do you confront someone you love? Is it possible to do that without anger?

Chapter 9 - Elizabeth's father shared wisdom with his daughters about marriage. Has someone shared some valuable insight with you? Did it help you avoid difficulties? Elizabeth found an abandoned grave. Why do you think she felt so strongly about this?

Chapter 10 - Jen was concerned about Elizabeth's decisions. Can you find strength in any of her decisions? Elizabeth shared that she was being transferred to another floor and told of her supervisor's crazy assumption. Have you been accused of something you feel is incorrect? How do you think you would handle this?

Chaptcr 11 - Mr. Grcyson showcd incredible kindness and care for a muddy, exhausted Elizabeth. Has anyone assisted you when you were at your wits end? Have you helped someone else this way? Why are support people important to have? What kind of support would you welcome today?

Chapter 12 - Elizabeth worried about talking to tombstones. Do you think speaking concerns aloud is helpful? Do you like the name she chose for the abandoned baby?

Chapter 13 - Elizabeth couldn't avoid Reggie at work nor her attraction to him. How do you think she handled the encounter? Elizabeth said she felt "broken." Do you think moving away will help? Why/Why not?

Chapter 14 - Do you think Elizabeth did the right thing by leaving a woozy Mrs. Krebbson? Why is decision-making harder when we're struggling? Did you ever have to change jobs because of stress? Was it easy or hard to do? Do you think Elizabeth had been derailed by her own junk or someone else's?

Chapter 15 - Elizabeth started a new job. Do you think a nursing home was a good choice for her? When Elizabeth was no longer able to escape her memories and was overwhelmed with grief. Why do you think she asked Hope to not hate her?

Chapter 16 - Elizabeth confided in Jen about her daily anxiety. How would you react if your best friend hid a struggle from you? Jen and Elizabeth shared similar experiences; yet, Elizabeth's response was vastly different. Can opinions change over time? Do you feel judged if someone else has a different opinion? If so, why?

Chapter 17 - Are there lessons in pain? Mr. Greyson saw Elizabeth's mother from an outsider's viewpoint. Is this helpful? Elizabeth's nurturing of a baby's grave sparked others to find solace in service. Why does helping others feel so good?

Chapter 18 - Were you excited to see Dr. Reggie at the cemetery with Elizabeth? She had decided to start counseling. How would you respond if a friend shared that information with you? In what way is counseling different than talking to a friend? How does forgiveness work? Is there more than one kind of forgiveness?

BONUS- An inside peek from
Mr. Greyson's childhood.

"Kenneth Samuel Grayson, what do you think you're doing?" His Gran had led him, by the ear, just around the corner of the General Store.

He gripped the hand causing his excruciating pain and tearfully cried, "Please let go." When she did he scanned the street for any bystanders that might have witnessed his embarrassing parade from the building, fortunately there were none. He tried to avoid his grandmother's piercing gaze and stammered, "I was just lookin' at it."

"Then how did it end up stickin' up outta your pocket?"

"Uh, I uh…" he stammered.

"Exactly! And I didn't raise no liar neither. Look up at me, son when I'm talking to you."

"Yes ma'am, Gran." He looked up quickly and saw the pain hiding behind her anger before refocusing on the tip of her slender nose.

"The Good Book says, "Thou shall not steal. Are you a thou?"

"Yes ma'am."

"Is that harmonica in your pocket rightly yours?"

A young couple passed by the small alley and looked on in curiosity. Kenneth looked down and shuffled his feet. "I uh…"

"I asked you to look at me, Kenneth, and do not lie. Is that harmonica rightly yours?"

"No ma'am, Gran," he said, looking back at the tip of her nose as it glinted in the sunlight.

"Ok then. Hand it over!" He slid it out quickly, and placed it in her opened hand. Reading the price tag, she said, "Twenty-five cents!" Yanking her handbag open, she snipped, "I am rightly ashamed of you young man."

His head dropped to his chest.

"You know that God provides for those who love and obey him. Disobedience like this will only bring pain. Look at me," she said sharply.

He quickly obeyed, this time he found softness in her face. She looked him clear in the eye as his thirteen-year-old body had surpassed hers in height two years prior. "I am your elder, and I am responsible for you. You will walk back into that store with this money." She handed him some coins. “You apologize and pay for it. You make that apology good. Thieves end up in jail or worse.” Her voice had grown sharp again, but he didn’t look away. “Mr. Peterson is a hardworking man. You understand that taking things from his store is like taking food away from his family. Did you consider that?”

“No ma’am, Gran.” His chin dropped a bit.

Her voice softened again and she sighed. “Looks like we’ll be eating lean this week unless someone can catch us a few rabbits.” He looked up with hopeful eyes. “Kenneth, this is the time you must make a decision on your path. The temptations of this world are like shiny gold, but they has an invisible hook that leaks poison into a soul. The only way we can battle Satan is with the power of God. You understand me, son?”

He nodded.

“You know I raised you better than this. You gonna let a hankerin’ for shiny tune-stick keep you from honoring God?” The air grew thick with the dust of a buggy passing by on the main road. “When we get home, you need to talk to God about this.” She handed him back the harmonica. “Now you go in and pay for it, and then you give that tune-stick back to me. It’ll be mine as I’m the one paying for it.” She gave him a little push, “Now go, and remember to tell him you’re sorry for leaving without paying.”

“Yessum, Gran,” he said quietly as he walked past her and went back into the store.

#

Kenneth sat on a fallen tree out behind their hand-hewn log home, grateful his Gran had let him sit out of doors to think. His gangly legs were long, and his knees stuck up higher than his waist. He inhaled the fragrance of the pine trees nearby, and his thoughts went to his last Christmas with his parents. Momma had been cooking up pheasant in the kitchen. He was sitting beneath the Christmas pine when his daddy came in from the double-stalled shed that housed their cow and horse. The smell of animal dung and hay on his daddy’s clothes were easily ignored as the aroma of a sweet mince pie cooling on their table had his full attention.

Momma made some small talk as her husband grabbed a rag and wiped barn residue off his boots. Kenneth was too busy thinking about the candy he'd get in his morning stocking to pay much attention, but when his daddy crossed to the kitchen with a look of concern on his face he set aside the anticipation of tomorrow's pleasure, and paid attention.

"Margaret's boy just came by, she's lookin' for ya. Time for the baby," he said quietly.

Momma's face blanched, "So soon?" Daddy nodded, and momma quickly wiped her hands on her apron and went into the bedroom.

"We're headin' out. Get your coat, son. All you boys, get your coats on. I'll drop you off at Gran's on the way." The memory of the 15-minute ride on the little buggy sitting between his parents with a partially cooked pheasant at his feet and all his brothers riding in the back brought mixed pleasure.

After a night filled with sugar sweet dreams, he awoke to his Gran's tear-streaked face. "Kenneth, your momma and daddy won't be coming for ya. They went to be with Jesus last night."

Being almost five years old, he didn't understand it. After their burial Gran moved into his parents' place with all five boys. He had heard her grumble about 'living in a house full of boys' every once in a while, but she never spoke of his parent's death.

When he was seven, Kenneth overheard his oldest brother talking to the smithy. "Yup, heard tell it was a spooked horse. A passing rider found them 'neath their buggy."

Kenneth now sat on a log, thinking about how he and his brothers had been spared while his parents 'went to Jesus.' Then words his Gran spoke this very day, as they walked home from the mercantile came to mind. "He who believes in me will never perish, but have an everlasting life."

Kenneth already knew about Jesus being God's Son, but Gran said there was more. "He who confesses his sin…" *Like my taking the harmonica?* "You know, I am sorry I did that, God. I didn't mean to hurt Mr. Peterson nor Gran," he said quietly. "Gran said you can help me be stronger than my temptations. Oh God, I do want that. I know there must be a reason you left me here when you took my parents. I'd rather follow you every day than let invisible hooks leak poison into my heart. Please help me to be strong and to want the things you want for me. I'm asking like Gran said, 'Jesus be my Shepherd,' please. Amen."

I hope I did it right. Kenneth looked up at their summertime garden and noticed a red fox slipping away into a grove of trees. He eyed their chicken coop on the other side of the field. "You run, you sly thing. There'll be no more stealing going on here!" *Yes sir, no more stealing going on here.*

*****

CPSIA information can be obtained
at www.ICGtesting.com
Printed in the USA
BVHW031008041222
653418BV00014B/760